THANK YE, MISTER SUN

R. H. RIFFENBURGH

Copyright © 2025 by R. H. Riffenburgh

All rights reserved.

No part of this book may be reproduced in any form or by any electronic or mechanical means, including information storage and retrieval systems, without written permission from the author, except for the use of brief quotations in a book review.

Published by Konstellation Press, San Diego

www.konstellationpress.com

Copy Editor: Lisa Wolff

Cover design: Scarlet Willette

Dedicated to the memory of my parents, Dr. Harry and Ada Riffenburgh, who were the models for the Hillson parents in the story

1

JULY 1939

We was in the cornfield when we seen him doin' that.

"Who's that?" Harry whispered. He stopped pullin' the dark brown corn silk off the ears.

"Julian Martin. He's a grad student. My pa is doing the farmwork for his fertilizer exper'ment," I whispered back.

Harry lifted his head up to see better, but couldn't cuz he was standin' in a furrow. I could see cuz I was standin' on a clod.

"What is he doing?" Harry asked, a little too loud. Harry talked more formal, cuz he was a faculty kid while I was a farm kid. I put my finger up in front of my mouth. He nodded and stuffed the corn silk in his pocket.

"He does re-search for a doctor degree. I think

he's trying to see if his new kine of fertilizer grows plants better'n the reg'lar kine. I guess if he shows his new thing grows better corn, he gets all rich and stuff."

"It sounds like he's not an army cadet here at VPI," Harry said.

"Naw. I said he's a grad student. It's them as ain't finished their college edication what're caydets and wear fancy uniforms."

"I know that, Ronson," Harry said. "That's how the school gets money from the government. It trains undergraduates to be military officers. A student has to get special permission to avoid being a cadet. But what's he doing?"

"I seen his special corn out in another field. It ain't growin' no better'n this here reg'lar. It looks to me like he's lettin' little bugs or worms or somethin' out of a jar into the reg'lar corn. It looks like he lets the critters mess up the corn so's it don't grow as good as it could."

"But that doesn't sound like a fair experiment," Harry said, soundin' all bothered.

"No, it don't," I said.

Julian was lookin' left and right like to make sure nobody saw what he was doin'. But he didn't see us. The corn is taller than us and I stood pretty still, like I do when I'm watchin' a bird or a rabbit. It was a hot day for summer in Blacksburg cuz usually days in the summer are pretty just right.

But that day was as hot as the shop where they teach students to weld. Uncle Sedgwick said it was as hot as a horzcunt, but I don't know what that is.

Anyway, the sun was shinin' down between the stalks and I was gettin' all sweaty, startin' to itch. The smell of the corn and the fertilizer was gettin' strong and I could hear a couple squawky crows fussin' at Julian for runnin' them off. I'd have given a heap for a breeze. But we didn't move.

Then Harry started to pull more of the dark brown corn silk off the ends of the corn.

"Harry," I said, "we better be gettin' outta here."

"But we haven't gotten much silk," Harry said. "That's what we came for."

That's why we was in the cornfield. We's both thirteen and can't buy cigarettes, so we roll the sunburnt silk up in a piece of an old *Roanoke Times*. Seems like everbody smokes. I guess a lot of the older folks don't, but, gee, all the young guys do. I mean it's nineteen and thirty-nine now and I'm modern. But my pa, he don't let me smoke. He says nobody in our Allen fambly should smoke. Only he can't stop Uncle Sedge. Me, I'd hide out behind the barn and smoke my corn silk. It made my head spin, but, what the heck, I'm almost grown up. It'd wear off in a few minutes and I could walk straight agin even though my stomach still hurt a little.

"Naw," I said. "We got enough. We gotta go. S'pose Julian catches us."

"He's way down at the other end of the row, Ronson. It will take a while for him to get back up here."

My stomach began to get tight. I was gettin' all nervous. "Harry," I said, sharp-like, "don't argue with me. We're goin'."

"Who made you my boss, Ronson Allen? Who? Who?"

"Harry Hillson," I said, louder than I should, "I know you're my bes' friend. I know you don't care that your pa teaches and my pa works the fields. I ain't tryin' to boss you. I'm just ascared my folks will get in trouble if we get caught spyin'."

Julian had went down the row droppin' a couple of bugs on one stalk and a couple more a few stalks farther on. He done turn around when he got to the end of the row and was comin' up toward us. So I grabbed Harry's arm and we slipped out. The fields is pretty big and by the time he got to the end of the row, we was gone. We didn't need that much corn silk and I done got my pocket full anyway.

We walked toward Harry's house. When we was far enough away, Harry asked, "How does putting worms on the corn affect his experiment?"

"He's got a special fertilizer mix in some fields and a ordinary mix in different fields. This here field is a ordinary one. I think puttin' worms in his ordinary field will make it do worse and make his pet fertilizer look good. I know about this stuff cuz when I help Pa in the fields, he tells me what they's doin' so I'll help him right."

Harry's eyes got big, then squinted as he frowned.

"That's cheating. It won't be a fair experiment. What should we do?"

"Aw, heck, Harry. We's just kids. We can't do nuthin'."

Harry was a little excited over it. He was breathin' hard and nodded when he said a word louder to make it sound stronger.

"We have to. We can't let the experiment give a false answer from cheating."

Harry used big words a lot. He wasn't tryin' to show off. It's just the way his family talked. Harry's pa, Doctor Hillson, taught chemistry and did exper'ments in groundwater hydrology—I think that's learnin' where the rain goes when it sinks in and how to get it back out and stuff—so he was always tellin' Harry about...about integrit...well, about being honest so's you can learn what's really going on on God's green earth—that's what Pa calls it. So Harry's just death on cheatin'.

"We *have* to do something," Harry went on, real worked up like. His eyes was big and he was breathin' so fast he started snortin' like a angry bull.

"Well, *you* do it," I said.

"I can't go without you," Harry said. "You're the one who actually saw it. I couldn't see over the corn. We have to go together."

"I don't know," I said. "I could tell Pa, but then he'd ask what I was doin' out there in the field and then he'd get on to us smokin'."

I was gettin' nervous. I didn't want to mess with it. It didn't have nuthin' to do with me. But with Harry, it's like he gets a bee up his britches and can't let go 'til he gets it out.

We had got to Harry's backyard and sat in the tree that had blowed over in the big wind a couple of years ago. Most of its roots was sticking up in the air, some as tall as I was. But they was enough still in the ground that the tree went on livin'—all green with leaves floppin' around in the wind and branches that bent down when we sat on them and sprang up when we got off.

Harry lived just acrost on the east side of the cornfield—well, it was corn that year, maybe somethin' else next year. The row of little houses for the farm workers went along the west side of the field and the faculty houses started on the east side. His pa's house was like a mansion to me, like you could put three or four of our houses in it, but he said his pa didn't think it was big enough, said the school was stingy. Well, they was a lot more stingy to us. We never had enough room or enough food. My maw used to bring in some money cleanin' folks' houses, but in this depression, she can't find nobody who can afford to pay her.

"Well, whatta we do, Harry?"

"I don't know." He shook his head lookin' a little sad. "I just don't know. We have to ask somebody."

"Who?"

"I have no idea."

We sat, quiet for a while.

"I tell you what, Harry. I'll ask Uncle Sedgwick when I get home. He pretty much wants to do things right, but he ain't a stick-in-the-mud-can't-budge-a-inch like Pa."

"Is he your pa's brother or your ma's?"

"Pa's. His last name's Allen like mine."

We thought some more on it for a while but gave up and climbed up into the falled-over tree.

For a couple of years, Harry and I done play pretend in the tree. It turned into anything we wanted it to be. I was gettin' tired of those little games. Seemed to be kind of babyish. But Harry still hung onto it. I think he knew better, but he just didn't want to let go of the good times we done had.

So we turned our blowed-over tree into a airplane in our minds. Harry wanted to fly our airplane to France, however far that was. He said that that's where the Great War made airplanes go from big kite-looking things to real airplanes. All I knew about France, it was where Pa and Uncle

Sedgwick fought in the war. And, oh yeah, I'd heard a little song-thing some kids was singin'—"In the southern part of France where they don't wear pants …." I couldn't picture it myself.

Anyway, the war was a long time ago. My folks would have been young then. But why would we want to go to France? Harry was always thinkin' ways I didn't get. He said maybe we could develop the airplane to another level. I didn't get that neither.

Anyway, before we got anywhere, the whistle blew. The college's powerhouse has a emergency whistle and they test it every day at six on the dot. Y'all can hear it for miles. All the kids know they got to skedaddle home to eat dinner when they hear the whistle. So it blew and turned our airplane back into a tree and we climbed down to head home.

"Hungry time," Harry said.

"What're y'all havin' for eats?" I asked.

"I don't know," he said. "Whatever my mom fixes. Last night we had pork chops, mashed potatoes with pork gravy, and Swiss chard from our garden."

"Gawdamighty," I said, feelin' a little sad. "All we usually get is soup."

"Why is that?" Harry asked.

"My pa don't get a whole lot of pay. And they take a lot of it out to pay for the little house they give us. Even with Uncle Sedgwick's pay thrown in—he lives with us and works the fields with Pa—the only way we can afford meat more than on Sunday is to steal a bird from the chicken farm up on Chicken Hill. It's out near the railroad track, y'know."

"You steal a chicken?" Harry asked, soundin' all surprised and worried.

"They got more chickens than they kin count," I said. "They don't even notice. Even so, it's hard to do, cuz there's always folks feedin' them or cullin' or gettin' eggs in the daytime. And at night all the rich kids get their pa's car and park up there sparkin'."

Harry's mouth hung open a minute. Like stealin' was a new thought to him. Then we started runnin' home. At that age, it was more fun to run than walk. And it didn't take so long to get places.

"What's for dinner, Ma?"

"'Tater soup, Ronson boy, just like yestiddy." I wasn't surprised.

Elliedine—she's my big sister—piped up. "I found some huckleberries already ripe along the railroad track. Ma put them in. It'll make it taste different from yestiddy."

Elliedine is always tryin' to make things better. I

think I look up to her even more than I do Ma and Pa.

Ma cleaned off the kitchen table and we all sat around it: my pa and my ma and Elliedine—she's near fifteen—and Uncle Sedgwick and me, and Ma dished us up a ladle of soup each. I wished I could have two, but there was hardly enough to go around as it was. They always sat me at the corner of the table cuz I was the youngest. It made me wonder why tables all had four sides. Why couldn't they make a table with five sides so I could have one? Maybe table makers can't count bigger'n four.

After dinner, Uncle Sedgwick took Elliedine and me out for a walk cuz it was still light cuz it was summer. He said it was to walk off the dinner, but that warnt true. We didn't have enough dinner to walk off. I knew—they didn't know I knew—that it was to let Ma and Pa have a chance for a little sparkin'. They didn't get no chance at night cuz we had only one sleep room and all five of us slept there.

When Elliedine went off to pick some wildflowers, I saw my chance to ask Uncle Sedg about the cheatin'.

"Uncle Sedgwick? I got a thing I want to ask you about."

He stopped walkin' and looked at me kind of hard. It must have been the way I said it. Uncle Sedgwick's body is kind of thick, well, with muscles, not fat. That's different from Pa, who's so thin his overhauls hang loose on him. It ain't that Pa is weak. He ain't as strong as Uncle Sedgwick, but he can keep on workin' after Sedgwick gets all tired.

"What's itchin' yer mind, Ronson?"

I told him about what Julian was doin'. He stood still, starin' at the pebbles stuck in the tar on the edge of the road for a minute. The tar was gettin' soft from the heat but wasn't hot enough yet to stick on our shoes.

"Ronson, it ain't our place to mess with what the college and its people does. Not our job. If we get hung up in it, they always blame us. We's too poor to fight back. They can shit on us and walk away and we get blamed for having shit on us. Ye get what I'm saying? Yer paw and me, we might even lose our jobs if you make a stink over it. Rightin' somebody else's wrong ain't worth me and yer pa losing our jobs. So let them have their own rot in their edication. Leave it alone. Like you didn't never see it, OK?"

I s'pose that made sense. It didn't seem right. But things is never right for the poor. It seems like money is strength and if you don't have it, you're weak and they can use you. Pa says the poor is like a flashlight battery to the rich—they buy you, use you, and throw you away when you're used up. But I don't think it's right.

After Uncle Sedgwick had gone on back to the house, Elliedine and I sat up near the water tower on the stump of a tree what had been cut down cuz its roots was pushin' up the edge of the road. The heat of the day had edged out slow like steam from a kettle took off the fire and now the cool of the evenin' was sneakin' in to take its place. Everthing had gone so quiet ye could hear the cloth of our shirts crinkle when we moved.

Elliedine snuggled her shoulders up around her neck and looked so happy I had to feel happy, too. She pushed her pretty lips out like she was kissin' the air.

"I jes' love this time of night, Ronson," she whispered. "It's the just-right time when you feel woke up from the heat and feel so alive. I feel like I could do anything when it's like this."

"Yeah, Ellie," I said. "I feel it, too." And I shivered a little and rolled my head in a circle just cuz I had to move somethin'.

The sun had got big and red as it neared the tops of the mountains. I waited for it to hit the highest mountain. I imagined how the sun might go all flat when it did. Or maybe how it would knock the top off the mountain or light it on fire or somethin'. We watched it go lower and lower and then touch the top. But nuthin' happened. It just slipped behind the mountain like always.

When there was only a little sliver of it left, I

stood up and called out to it so it would know we was glad it had come to see us today and would come back tomorrer.

"Good night, Mister Sun," I said real loud so he could hear. Elliedine giggled at my little game and stood up too. It was time to go home.

THE NEXT DAY Harry and I took our BB guns and went out into the woods behind Harry's house. The woods was just great. They was thick woods like what they call a forest. There was birds and all kinds of animals—possums and foxes and stuff. We shoot our guns at them, but it's like they knows it's just in fun and don't pay no attention. Harry and I shoot each other in the back sometimes. At twenty foot it stings a little but couldn't really hurt nuthin'. At forty foot, like when we aim at a bird or animal, it'd jes' be like gettin' brushed by a bush. Wouldn't hurt nuthin'. And anyway, the BB drops down before it goes that far. I've tried aimin' higher so it hits when it drops down, but I never know how high to aim and I never hit nuthin'.

One time Harry did hit a bird—a robin. It fell down and flopped around. He didn't know that birds flop after they're dead. I seen Pa kill a chicken and it flopped around half a acre before it stopped. He says it's just the nerves kickin' up the muscles after it's dead. I guess that's right. It can't be alive after its head is chopped off. But Harry didn't know about that and he was mighty bothered. My ma would say he was beside hisself, but that don't make no sense to me. How can a body be beside itself? Harry cried and cried and wouldn't shoot at anything for at least a month.

We scrunched down and pushed ourselves through the hole in the fence leadin' to the woods. It was cool and you couldn't hear nuthin' except when a bird would sing. Harry said the leaves and brush absorbed the sound waves, but I don't get what he means.

After maybe a half hour we got to the railroad track where this patch of woods ended. Our folks always told us not to walk on the tracks cuz we could get hit by the train. Y'all think this black thing almost as big as a house comes up getting bigger and bigger each second and says choo-choo-choo louder and louder and we wouldn't have enough sense to get off the track? Adults is just unreal sometimes.

Harry didn't want to walk the track cuz he'd been told not to, but I dared him, so he done it. We walked on the rails, him on one side and me on the other, to see who could walk the farthest without fallin' off. I won. I always did. Harry just wobbled a little and then more and then finally too much. We heard the train comin'. Harry had a penny. It was a

Indian head penny. They was some still around even though they'd changed the Indian to Mister Lincoln way back before even Uncle Sedgwick could remember. Harry put it on the track and we hid behind a tree so the engineer wouldn't see us and know we was up to somethin'.

The train went past like a peal of thunder, throwin' out steam and oil drops. Ye could smell the oil and burnt coal. We couldn't help being a little scared it was so big and loud, but it was a sort of a thrill scare and was good. It went down the track. Its sound was lower goin' away than when it was comin'. Harry said it was cuz it pushed the sound when it was comin' and pulled it away when it was goin'. I don't see how it could do that.

We couldn't find the penny at first. Finally I spotted it three or four feet down between two ties. It was squashed real thin, longer up and down than side to side. The Indian's head was all stretched out and his feathers was super long.

People made fun of the train, callin' it a little switcher engine. It didn't go very fast. People called the train the Huckleberry, cuz you could get off the front and grab a handful of huckleberries that grew all along the track and get back on the back as it went by. It ran back and forth eight miles from Blacksburg to Christiansburg, the nearest place where the big Norfolk and Western hunnert-car coal trains ran through, and it carried food and supplies to Blacksburg and coal back out. It went frontwards one way and backwards the other cuz there wasn't no way to turn it around.

One time Harry's ma bought tickets and took him to Christiansburg and back so he could see what a train ride was like. My ma didn't have no money for that.

"Harry," I said, "I asked my uncle Sedgwick about the cheater. He said rich folks make their own problems, so should take care of them theyselves. We should stay out of it. He says it ain't our place. He says he and Pa might get laid off if'n we make a stink."

"But then Julian will get away with it, Ronson. That's not right. And anyway, what is our 'place'? We don't have a 'place.' That's for countries like India. I heard my dad telling about people there called 'untouchables' that have to say 'unclean' if you get too close to them. They have to do the dirtiest jobs and don't get paid enough to live on."

I thought about that for a bit. People even poorer than we are. I don't believe it. "That's just gossip, Harry. They ain't no folks like that."

"Well, my dad says Professor Markov says so."

I felt right riled. I spoke mean to Harry, which I never do.

"I asked Uncle Sedgwick what 'pro-fessor' meant. He says it means they profess, which means they claims things but don't really know. It's what Uncle Sedg would call 'bullshit,' Harry."

"Right or wrong, we can't let someone cheat on science."

"Right or wrong, Uncle Sedgwick says they'll put the blame on us if we gets into it. He says if'n they can't find their way out of their own mess, let'm stew."

Harry didn't seem to have any more to say. He picked up his BB gun and started back toward home. So I did the same. We went back to Harry's house, which was at the edge of the woods, and we made a fort in the sandbox they had put in their back yard.

Harry had some neat soldiers made out of solid lead. They was American made, so was pretty strong. He had a couple of sailors made in Japan. They cost two for a nickel instead of a nickel each like the American ones, but they was hollow tin and thin and broke easy. Once we bent one open after it broke and it said Campbell Soup on the inside! Americans sent old cans to Japan and they made soldiers out of them and sold them back to us. That seemed pretty smart, but I'd rather have one strong one we could shoot off the wall of the fort with a slingshot than two what just broke. Everthing that comes out of Japan is just flimsy.

"Harry," his ma called. "I'm making bread. Would you please come in and knead the dough?"

They had a big pot with a crank on the top hooked to a blade inside that turned dough around and mixed it over and over. My ma had to do it with her hands.

I stayed outside. I never felt quite right inside. Harry's ma and pa were nice to me. They asked how I was and did I want somethin' to eat and stuff, but I always felt like they was bendin' over for me. I don't quite know how to say it. Like they was bein' good to me cuz they felt sorry for me. I didn't want no one to feel sorry for me. I didn't feel sorry for myself. I had a ma and pa what go without to give me enough and a uncle what teaches me things and a sister as sweet as sugar on choc'lit, and most days food to eat and the sunshine and the forest to go watch animals. What did I have to feel sorry for? And if I didn't feel sorry, why should they? Well, anyway, my pa, he said they is damnyankees and you can't trust them no matter how nice they is to me.

After a while, Miz Hillson came out and spoke to me.

"Hello, Ronson, how are you today?"

"Jes' fine, ma'am," I said.

"Well, that's good to hear. Say, we have accumulated more eggs than we can use." The Hillsons raised chickens. "Can I send some to your mother?"

Ma wouldn't want to take what she calls charity.

But then I thought eggs for breakfast. Startin' the day with somethin' in my stomach. And eggs! I thought fast. How could I make it look to Ma that it wasn't charity?

"Miz Hillson, ma'am, if I could do something for you in return? Something to help out?"

Miz Hillson put her hand on her chin and looked off at the big oak where a bluebird was singin' and a couple of squirrels was chatterin'. Then she nodded. She seemed to understand.

"Yes, we do need someone to deliver the cartons of eggs to the neighbors we have promised them to."

I knew that was usually Harry's job, but here was a chance to tell Ma I earned the eggs through chores.

"Yes, ma'am. I'll go get Pa's bicycle and do it."

"Oh, I think Harry will let you use his bike. It has a basket. Won't you, Harry?"

"Sure," said Harry. "You can do it and I won't have to."

I was gone to deliver the eggs when Doctor Hillson came home. Harry told his pa what we seen and his pa said the same thing Harry said: it ain't right. He said science has to be done honest and everbody has to know everthing what was done. He said we should go tell Julian's p'fessor about it. That'd be the right thing to do. But he told one thing to Harry hard like a hammer—we don't say why Julian was doin' it, that is, what we think is going on. We say only what we seen exact and no more. It's up to the p'fessor to decide the why.

The idea of talkin' to the p'fessor made me as nervous as a mouse looking up at the grin of a king snake. I was scared to do the wrong thing and maybe get Pa in trouble. But Harry wouldn't listen to me.

"Ronson, we have to do it. We just have no choice if we want to keep our self-respect."

I thought about it. Maybe if, like Harry's pa says, we just say what we seen and don't say what it means, then it couldn't get Pa and Uncle Sedgwick in trouble. But I didn't feel happy.

"Well, maybe, Harry. But tell me who his p'fessor is and what we say to him."

"I don't know who he is. Oh, gee! I wouldn't know what to say to him. Would he listen to us, just kids? If he didn't believe us, it would just make us look like the dishonest ones."

"Yeah, it would. I don't like it. Maybe Uncle Sedgwick is right. I tell you what, Harry, when you know who and what to say, I'll listen."

Harry hung his head like he'd got a broke neck. He was lookin' at the floor.

"I don't know, Ronson. I just don't know."

I went home.

When I gave the eggs to Ma and told her I'd earned 'em by doing chores, her face all wrinkled up in a smile like I hadn't seen since I brought home a report card from school with a bunch of Satisfactories on it. I'd had too many Unsatisfactories 'til then. See, the grade school in Blacksburg don't give A's and B's and stuff, just S's and U's.

"Sedgwick helped some visitors at the William Preston Hotel with their car what got a flat tire and he got a tip," Ma said. "It was a whole quarter. Take Pa's bicycle and go down to the Piggly Wiggly and get some sausage."

She give me the quarter and a poke to tote the sausage back in.

"Tomorree we're goin' to have sausage and eggs for breakfast!"

You can bet I was on that bike in half a minute. Sausage and eggs for breakfast. It was like Christmas!

2

AUGUST 1939

Elliedine would turn fifteen this month. I knowed Ma would bake her a cake when her birthday come aroun' and Pa would buy food for a special dinner. Uncle Sedgwick would likely give her some piece of clothes, maybe a pretty new shirt—she'd been growin' out of her clothes and lots of them was too small for her. So what could I do for her? I thought and thought 'til my head hurt and got nuthin' thunk. I didn't have no money and didn't know a way to get enough to buy her nuthin'. She sometimes got a baby-sittin' job and come home with a couple dimes, so even she had a little money. When I turned thirteen, she give me a whole tube of BBs so's I could go off in the woods and shoot with Harry, although they was the cheap lead kind 'stead of the copper kind Harry had. The lead ones didn't go so far cuz they was heavier. And they had a faster drop, so you had to guess how much higher to point the BB gun to hit somethin'. But even so, I done about as good as Harry. Anyway, she had done got me a present on my birthday.

I didn't want to get her somethin' just to pay her back. That would be mean. I wanted to get her a present cuz I loved her more'n anybody in the world and cuz she never 'spected nuthin' from nobody. A present always made her so happy.

I wondered what she'd like. Well, it got pretty clear to me that if I was goin' to have somethin' to give her, I'd have to make it. But I didn't have no stuff to make somethin' out of. And anyway, what could I make? I thought and thought. After a while I had a idea. She still loved dolls. I figgered I'd have to get her to let on to what kind of doll she'd like without her knowin' that was what I was doin'.

So next time Ma sent her downtown to get some food we was out of, I tagged along. I didn't want to mess with the food stuff, so I just stood by the door and waited. I watched her. Everbody likes to watch Elliedine, cuz she just naturally walks like a movie star. She don't move jerky like. She moves all smooth and easy like a eagle swoopin' down or a deer runnin' across a field. I guess there's a word for it, but I don't know it. Probably Harry'd know one. In fact, one time he did call her "grasefull" or somethin' like that, but I never heard that word before. 'Course, if I told her that folks watched her, she'd just turn all red and tell me I was the silliest boy in tarnation.

Anyway, she's real slim and I always get the feel she'd break like a china statue if you touched her, but she doesn't. Maybe it's cuz she is real gentle-like herself. But when I do somethin' nice, she hugs me real strong and she can do hard work with Ma that shows she ain't fra-gile.

"Elliedine," I says when we was leavin' Kroger's on Main Street, "let's go to Roses Five and Dime and look at stuff."

She stopped and looked at me all curious like.

"You ain't got no money, Ronson."

"Yeah, I know I don't. I just like to look at things. You know, see what sort of things folks is makin' and usin' these days. And some of them got all sorts of pretty colors and you can feel all sort of feels—soft and hard and fuzzy and stuff."

She looked at me some more, kind of surprised lookin'.

"I never thought about it like that, Ronson. OK, let's look and see what new things are bein' made and what colors they are and what textures they have."

Oh. "Textures." That's the word I needed.

We went a few doors down the street to Roses. The smell when we walked in always hit me like a bucket of cold water—a mix of dust and some kind of cleaner stuff. I led her down the left aisle all the way to the back of the store and then back down the other aisle, stoppin' to make like I was lookin' at everthing. But all the while, I was watchin' her out of the corner of my eye. I wanted to see what would make her light up. Whenever she stopped, I was careful to hang back so's not to hurry her. Mebbe there's somethin' else what I could make for a present.

She picked up some clothes and looked at sizes. She held up a shirt—she called it a blouse. I can't figger why girl-folks have to have different words for things. And another thing I can't figger is why they's so interested in clothes. You cover yourself up and stay warm and what more is there? Well, lookin' for a present, clothes didn't strike no bell, cuz I couldn't make none.

And then farther on she stopped and looked at some makeup things, lipstick and like. OK, I just got to keep sayin' it. I don't get it. Why, when she's purty as a picture all natural, does she think she's got to paint herself? Mebbe it's cuz the movie stars do it. But why do they do it? But, then, even Ma puts a little on herself when she dresses up to go to church. Well, Ma is older and skinnier and gettin' creases in her face like a plum startin' to dry toward a prune, so I kin see why she might do it. But Elliedine? I just don't get it. Anyway, it didn't ring no bell. I couldn't make no makeup.

But then, when we got to the other side of the store, she stopped and looked at some dolls. This was what I come for. I remembered how she still had a doll what Grandma had give her when she was little. She doesn't never play with it no more, but she kept it and loved it.

"Elliedine," I says, "do you still like dolls?"

"Sure, Ronson. I don't get no fun playin' house with them and all, but I like to have them around. It makes the world seem like a kinder place, I guess."

Ding dong. The bell done rung. I was on the right track.

She didn't go for the dolls what was all molded and hard and looked real except that they's little. She went for a Raggedy-Ann doll and held it up and kissed it before she put it back. She didn't want a model of a person. She wanted a cloth doll all floppy and loveable. I done hit the jackpot.

To play my part, I asked her why some of the cooking pots had reddish bottoms. She said it was copper and heated up faster but cost more. Then I looked at a BB pistol—Harry and I just had BB rifles—and also looked at some lead soldiers and at some toy airplanes. They didn't have two-winged airplanes like the only ones we see flyin' around here, but they had a one-winged one with a engine on each wing like the big ones what carry people out of the airport at the big city of Roanoke.

Roanoke is forty miles away and I've heard it has sixty thousand people in it.

When we got to the end of the second aisle, we just walked out.

"Thank ye, Ellie," I said. "That was fun."

"Yes, it was, Ronson. It makes me remember some of the fun we had together when we was little. Let's do this again sometime after a while when they get new stuff in."

And we walked home together, brother and sister, feelin' all close in a family way. Ain't it funny how you can feel like you're hooked together when you ain't even touchin'?

Well, I had to figger out how to make a doll. I thought through everthing I could get my hands on to start one. There were branches and logs out in the woods. Mebbe I could carve one. But the wood was hard and I didn't have no tools. It would take months to carve one down with just a pocketknife. Large bones from carcasses? They's even harder. And she didn't want a hard doll anyway. A lot of dolls is made from sewin' heavy cloth in the shape of the skin and stuffin' them with cotton or somethin'. But I don't got no money to buy that kind of cloth or stuffin'. And most likely I couldn't sew good enough anyways.

Then I hit on it. A ear of corn. Young corn had a big supply of yellow corn silk growin' out of the top that could be yellow hair. That could be the head. The lower part of the shucked ear itself could be the body. I could take baby corn ears, shuck and scrape them, and sew them on for arms and legs. I could borrow a needle and thread from Ma. I had a old underwear shirt startin' to get holes. I could cut that up in shapes and prob'ly sew enough to make a dress.

But what could I do for a face? A doll with no face ain't no good at all.

I slept on it for a couple of nights, goin' over and over ideas in my mind. But I was sure I would come up with somethin', so I started collectin' materials during the day. I went out into the cornfields and found a huge ear of corn with a fine head of hair. I could cut it down and shape it to fit what I planned. Findin' little bitty corn ears for arms and legs was easy. I shucked and cooked and carved and got it all ready. I couldn't boil the big one cuz that would ruin the hair, so I stuck it on a ice pick and held it in the boilin' pot with the top of the head over the side so's the steam wouldn't get to the hair.

Then I borried—well, snuck—Ma's biggest needle and strongest thread and sewed the arms and legs on. I took my old undershirt and laid it out and drawed with a pencil where I wanted to cut to make a dress. Then I sewed the top layer to the bottom layer all around the edge just inside the cut line. I cut it and turned it inside out so's the stickin'-out edges wouldn't show. Fine. It worked. Mebbe I'd get a little cold on some days next winter without the undershirt, but it'd be worth it.

I looked at the dress and shook my head. Somethin' wasn't right. It was just all white. I wanted some color to make it look like a girl's dress. I couldn't get colors or nuthin' from the vocational training class cuz there wasn't no school. It's summer. Finally, I snuck a little red bottle of fingernail color from Elliedine's box of stuff and touched it here and there with the tip of the brush. Breathin' the fumes from the bottle made me a little dizzy, sort of like when I snuck that cornsilk smoke. Did girls get all dizzy when they painted their fingernails? Anyway, it looked pretty good with all them red polka dots. I figgered it might turn dark with time, but that didn't matter. You see all colors of polka dots. The arms I'd sewed on was all floppy, so I didn't have no trouble fittin' the dress on the doll body.

I wasn't no closer to a face. The doll looked real good, well, good to me, except that the face part looked like it had been run over by a itty-bitty threshin' machine.

Next time I was downtown for somethin', I went back in to Roses and looked at their dolls. I hoped I wouldn't see none of the other kids from school, me looking at girls' dolls. I touched the face of one. It was hard, like a clay pot! Was it clay what'd been painted over? Oh, boy, was I iggorant about dolls! Here I'd been thinking of a soft face, like the Raggedy Ann doll. But my doll wasn't floppy soft and it wasn't statue hard. My idea was somethin' in the middle between a hard doll and a soft doll. A hard face with a stiff body, but soft and floppy on the outside with floppy arms and legs. Soon as I had my idea, I skedaddled away from the dolls quick as a woodchuck duckin' a houn' dog.

Well. Clay. But school was out. Where could I get clay? I cornered Uncle Sedgwick that evenin' when he got home.

"Uncle Sedgwick, does the college have vocational trainin' courses, like public school?"

"Not really, Ronson. Why you askin'?"

"Can you keep a secret?" I asked. He began to look all closed up wary, like a coon hearin' a gun bein' cocked.

"Depends," he says.

"Nuthin' bad," I says. "Just a surprise for Elliedine's birthday. I don't want her to hear about it."

"Oh, then, sure," he says, with his face goin' softer. I couldn't help but think how mean Uncle Sedg looked when he was worried. When he was all bothered, his heavy eyebrows done come together. And then, I thought how friendly he looked when he wasn't worried. Sort of nice-guy lookin'. How can a feelin' inside change how you look at the world so much?

"I'm tryin' to make somethin' for her and I need some clay like they make pots out of."

"You makin' a pot for her?"

"Aw, no, Uncle Sedg, a doll. I need to make a doll face."

"I see," he says, bitin' his upper lip with his lower teeth and lookin' up at the ceiling. I thought how even his teeth were. Pa's was a little crooky, and they was brothers. Why would the good Lord give one kid somethin' nice and his brother not? I thought the good Lord must have a little mean streak or else an awful strange sense of humor. After a few seconds, Uncle Sedg answered. "They got a materials lab with every kind of material you can think of for when they might need it in an experiment. I bet they'd have somethin' like that. I know the technician over there. I'll ask him tomorrie when I go over to work."

Well, would you believe it? The next day Uncle Sedgwick brought home a little bag of brown powder.

"This here's air-dry clay you don't have to fire in a kiln. You mix it with water. It starts settin' up right away, but you have time enough to mold it.

Then you have to wait two or three days for it to dry complete before you use it."

I mixed the powder with water. I added a little bit at a time, like cookin' cornmeal, cuz you can always add more, but you can't take none out once it's in. When I could shape it and it would hold that shape, I made a head around the top of the corn cob and then tried to shape the face. I squoze the clay up for nose and cheeks and chin and stuff and pushed it down for eyes below the eyebrows and like that. I made a bulge across the lower part and shaped it into lips usin' a little stick I had whittled the end on to look like a screwdriver. I didn't do real well, I have to say. I ain't had no practice with clay and I ain't had no practice with art. I can't just paint it to look like a face. I put it aside to dry and thought maybe I'd have to give it up. It just looked too childish.

Well, by the time it dried hard, I had thought of a way to get around my mess. I'd take some more of my undershirt and glue it to the face. That'd make it white and cover it up some. There was glue in the tool storage room in the barn where Pa worked. They'd never miss one little bottle.

I glued the cloth on with the little brush that came in the glue bottle and pushed it down into the creases with my whittle stick. After that, it looked better. We had ink in the house and I made a pen out of a large tail feather from a dead chicken. I drew eyes and eyebrows and holes under the nose and curlicues in the ears. Then I used Elliedine's nail polish agin to make red lips. When I was done, I thought it looked just awful. But it was only two days 'til Ellie's birthday and I was stuck. It'd have to do. I hoped somethin' was better than nuthin'. I wrapped it in newspaper and tied it with a string. I used the chicken feather what I'd cut into a pen and wrote "To Elliedine, with love, Ronson" in a blank space.

THE EVENIN' of Elliedine's fifteenth birthday, everthing went like I had thought it would. Ma cooked the dinner and Pa brought it in from the kitchen cuz he had bought all the special food. Then, after we ate, Ma brought in the cake she had baked and we all sang "Happy Birthday" and ate it. Then Uncle Sedgwick brought a package all wrapped up purty. Elliedine opened it and found a purty shirt—I mean blouse—just her size in a soft kind of cloth that had some kind of gussy name.

Well, it was time for me to bring my present if it ever was, so I brought out the package. It looked so cheap and childish after Uncle Sedgwick's package that I almost took it back. But nobody said how bad it looked and Ellie gave me that sweet smile of hers that hooks on to yer heart and squeezes it. She pulled off the wrappings and sat there lookin' at what would win a bet for the ugliest doll ever was.

I turned red and squoze down in my seat wishin' I could disappear, hopin' I would, but no such luck. Everbody looked at it and looked. Elliedine turned her head sideways and looked at the top and the side and the other side. Then she looked up at me and she had tears in her eyes.

Oh, Lordy, I thought. *She's so disappointed she's cryin'.*

She spoke. "Ronson, this is the most beautiful doll, the most perfect present I ever got."

"Aw, Ellie," I mumbled. "It's made awful." I couldn't look her in the face. I looked at the floor.

She jumped up and took me into her arms and hugged me and hugged me. Then she sat back down and hugged the doll.

"Ronson, I will keep this and treasure it for the rest of my life. I'll look at it every day. And every time I look at it, I will see that it's not a doll at all. It's a ...." She paused. She didn't know the right words. "It's a bucket of love. It says how much we love each other and will 'til the end of our days." The wet in her eyes overflowed and ran down her cheeks.

3

SEPTEMBER 1939

Everbody says they hate school, but I don't think they do. Some kids just want to keep on doin' what they was doin' all summer, but it seems to me like somethin' new is better after you done somethin' over and over. There's a lot of things I like about school. For one, you get new thoughts.

Well, it's September and school's startin' up agin. Harry and I ain't got no further in figgerin' out what to do about Julian Martin's cheatin'. But now our days is filled up and then we got homework to do. Harry's so careful about doin' his homework right after school that we don't get time to do much together. I'd rather do mine after the light's gone and I can't do nuthin' outside. Then I get to sit with Elliedine at the table while she does her'n. Somehow, bein' close to her makes me feel like I can do anything, even my homework. The closer ye sit to Elliedine, the more ... well, I can't say it right ... the more strong and soft you feel at the same time. And, maybe better, I get a full side of the table instead of a corner.

Anyway, after school the second week, Harry got to lookin' awful serious when we was walkin' home.

"Ronson," he says, "my dad told me something at breakfast. He said that autumn harvest is in progress and if we want to do something about Julian's cheating, we should do it without any more delay, before the evidence has been destroyed."

The way he said that was all highfalutin, like when the preacher says we gotta stop sinnin'.

"OK, Harry. What do we do, then?"

"Do you have any bright ideas?"

"Nope. Narry a one."

"Well, doggone it, Ronson, neither do I. I guess there's nothing to do but go to Julian's professor and tell him."

"Alright, Harry, y'all find out who he is and where he sits. I got nobody to ask who knows anything about the p'fessors."

"Yeah," says Harry, and he looks at the ground like he expects to read the answer down there. And there our problem lay day after day, festerin' and startin' to turn sour.

School was real different for us now. See,

Blacksburg has only seven grades before you go into four years of high school, so it was this year I started high school.

In grade school, you stay with the same teacher all day and she—yeah, she; they ain't no men teachers in grade school and precious few in high school—she teaches you all the different subjects. For the first four years in primary school, I was in the new brick building and then, for the next three, I moved over to the old one next door where the liberry is. It was supposed to be white, but had bluish showin' through where the paint was gettin' thin and a little gray all over from the dirt hangin' on to it.

I was glad to be gone from Miss Beeks. She's the principal of the grade school. All of us kids was scared of her. It ain't that she was mean. I never saw her be unfair. It was just that she didn't never take no foolishness from a kid. She had little round glasses and when she squinted at you through them, you wished you could be around the corner. When we left grade school last May, she was real nice and said nice things to all of us who was goin' acrost the schoolyard to the high school, but I knew that if I didn't behave like she wanted she'd still go all squinty at me. I was glad to go.

High school was different. Each hour, I'd go to a different room that had a different teacher to learn a different subject. The teacher for that subject knew a lot more about it than the grade school teachers did, but less about everthing else. I liked it that way. You could ask any question and get a good answer, not like the grade school where the teacher would sometimes lead you way around Robin Hood's barn without givin' you a straight answer cuz she didn't really know the full story.

The trouble was, the faculty kids knew almost everthing and some of the kids from the mines didn't know nuthin'. I'll tell you what that was like.

One day we was in Miss Florence Kipps's English class. Miss Kipps and her sister, Mae, were local folks and had taught there a lot a years. So she knew all the tricks to get the kids to be part of the class. See, the kids who didn't know nuthin' would rather be anywhere, maybe even down the mine, than there, cuz it made them feel dumb. When she would ask a question in class, the faculty kids' arms all went up like the stripey arm at a railroad crossin' after the train went by. But she didn't often call on them. She knew they knew the answer. She wanted to get to the kids shrinkin' down in their seats. Sometimes the faculty kids got so tired holdin' up their arms that they used their other arm to hold up the raised arm.

Anyway, Miss Kipps come across the word "craven" in a story she'd assigned us to read. She asked who knew what that meant. All the faculty kids' and a couple of the town kids' hands went up.

None of the country kids' did. That wasn't a word we used. She ignored all the hands and asked Archie, whose pa was a miner, if he knew.

"Nah, Miss Kipps. Ah don't," he said, all embarrassed. But she wanted to get past his wall into his mind.

"Well, Archie, do you think it's a good word or a bad word?"

"Ah don' know, ma'am."

"All right, let's look at it this way. If someone called you craven, would you be more likely to say 'Thank y'all very much' or would you say 'I gonna see ye out behind the barrn'?" She carried the r's out long in "barn." She knew better than to talk rough like that, but she sometimes did it so's the kids'd feel more at home.

Archie thought a minute and then said, "I'd say, 'Ah'll see ye out behind the barrn.'" He made a fist and bounced the knuckles off his nose.

"Right!" she said. "Good for you, Archie. You got it." She patted him on the back and then went back to the story. For about ten minutes, Archie sat grinnin' like a cat what caught a mouse. Some of the faculty kids rolled their eyes and looked at each other, but I thought she was a awful good teacher.

Well, days was goin' by pretty fast and Harry and I didn't think no more about Julian's cheatin'. Football season was startin'. Football was a big deal at Virginia Tech. On the night before a game, the caydets would build a pile of wood maybe twelve foot high, light it off, and stand around the fire singin' and yellin' school chants, like "Solerex! Soleri! Tech! Tech! VPI!" All the kids who lived near went there and stood aways back watchin' the fire and the caydets gettin' all worked up.

Then the Saturday of the game, a lot of people from outside came in their cars to watch. As they came up the hill on Clay Street from town, they passed the brick pillars markin' the start of campus. On the way to where you went into Miles Stadium, on the right side was the tree nursery right up to the stadium, but on the left was Harry's place with its big front yard. The week before, Doctor Hillson would get the school to send over the two garbage wagon horses and driver pullin' a big mower to cut the grass that had growed up to my knees. Then before the game, Harry and I would offer to let people park there for a nickel cuz there weren't but precious little parkin' around the stadium.

We made a big sign, measured off parkin' rows and columns, and put sticks in the ground to show boundries. With careful parkin' we could get a hunnert cars in there. That would bring in five whole dollars! Harry would stand out waving and callin' on the drivers to park there and I'd guide them into places. I walked in front to keep 'em slow so's their wheels wouldn't tear up the grass. Then

I'd squeeze 'em close so's we could get more cars in and get more nickels. Harry said he learned what to yell from what he called a shill he saw in a movie. He'd yell out, "Park your car here. Only a nickel, the twentieth part of a dollar," and stuff like that. I thought it sounded plum silly and I wouldn't do it.

We learned a lot about how to write signs about our business, about changin' money, about what a car could do and couldn't do, and, scariest, about what to say to people who didn't like how we did things, 'specially when they'd already opened their jug of moonshine or Kentucky whiskey.

Harry's folks didn't want to take any of the money for usin' their yard. They said we did the work, we get the profit. We split it. Harry put most of his in a box to buy things he wanted and I took most of mine to Ma. But Miz Hillson said we ought to use a little bit for somethin' fun to pay us back for all the work. So, on the Monday mornin' after the Saturday when we parked cars for the game, we each took a quarter and went to the creamery.

See, the college had a lot of milk and cream cuz they did exper'ments with raisin' cattle and teachin' students to run a dairy farm. And they also taught them how to bottle and sell and truck the milk and ice cream and all that stuff. They had what they called a creamery. We'd go there sometimes and the man in charge would sell us real cheap the best kind of things I ever ate—rich and sweet—with vanilla and choc'lit and all that. For our quarter, we ate all kinds of things, so much my stomach started to hurt.

It was late mornin' when we started home. We had just got to the top of the hill above the creamery when we heard a airyplane real loud, its engine stutterin' as bad as Billyjoe who can't talk good. We looked up and saw this two-wingy plane with yeller wings and a blue body comin' real low. It was one of the trainin' planes the college used at its airfield a few miles out of town. Harry said his pa told him they was made by a Mister Reuben Fleet up in Canada.

It come lower and lower and we could see it was goin' to land. Or maybe crash, cuz we was miles from the airport and there wasn't no place to land but the open field where we was standin'. Well, it come down almost hittin' the top of the chestnut oak tree we was standin' under. And the tree was less than a hunnert feet tall. There was a big open field beyond and it come down quick and bounced and stopped in the field.

The airyplane looked so little up in the sky. But, Lordy, did it seem big when it got close to us. And loud and whooshin'. We both ducked when it went past, even though it couldn't hit us through the tree. My heart was beatin' like a bunny rabbit's. You'd know what I mean if you'd ever held one. Was we ever excited? You bet we was!

We went runnin' over to it. The pilot climbed out of the cockpit carryin' a couple of tools and took off his helmet and goggles.

"What happened, Mister?" asked Harry. He was always more willin' to talk to grownups than I was.

"One of my cylinders seems to have lost its spark," he said, smilin'. I wondered why he was bein' so nice. I found out soon enough—he wanted our help. Which was OK. We was excited to be able to help him.

I knew a little about engines from working with my pa on the tractor he used in the farmin'. I could see the plane had five cylinders around in a circle in the front.

"Do you know where I could find a ladder or even a big box?" he asked.

"There's a ladder just up there in the chicken hatchery," I said. "Do y'all want me to get it?"

"That would help me so much," he said. And, then, to Harry, "While he's getting the ladder, would you help me clear the field?"

"Sure," Harry said, pleased as punch to have any part of this.

They started down the path the airyplane would use takin' off, lookin' for potholes or rocks that might snag a wheel, while I went to get the ladder. The ground was smooth enough and they moved a few rocks maybe the size of a melon over to near the fence. Then, I couldn't figger why, each carried one back.

I set the ladder up by the engine as they walked back. They put one rock in front of each wheel and I figgered out the pilot didn't want it to roll before he was ready. He climbed up the ladder and started takin' out the spark plugs one by one and feelin' the gap with a gauge. On the third plug, he yelled out.

"Ah-HA! I've found the culprit."

He fixed the gap, put back the plug, climbed down, and moved the ladder.

Harry worked up nerve and asked, "Were you scared, Mister?"

"I should say so, kid. Anytime you lose your power, you come down, whether you're over the ocean or over a forest or wherever. It was pure luck to find this field."

"I'm afraid I freeze up when I'm scared," Harry said.

"Well, if you freeze up in an aircraft emergency, you're dead."

"How can you keep from freezing up?" asked Harry.

"Why, kid, when you have a challenge you're scared of, you just have to take yourself in hand and find the courage to grab the bull by the horns."

With that, he climbed up on the wing, reached

into the cockpit, pushed some lever, and climbed back down.

"All right, I'll tell you boys what we're going to do. You two stand by the wheels, one on each side. I'm going to swing the propeller to start the engine. Then I'll go around and get in the cockpit, ready to take off. When I give you the signal, you push these rocks away from the wheels and then move out of the way.

"Now here's something very, very important. You don't move toward the front of the plane. If you do, the propeller will grind you up into mincemeat, understand? What you do is back up, keeping one hand touching the wing until you get to the end of the wing. Then back a couple steps farther and I'll take off. Got it?"

"Yessir," we said together.

Then he did and we did and off he went. We watched the plane go faster and faster, but it didn't go up. Finally, just before it reached the fence, it hopped up and rose over the trees and went higher and higher. I realized I'd been holdin' my breath. We whooped and jumped around a bit. We watched it get smaller and smaller and finally fade out of sight.

I picked up the ladder to take back on our way home. We walked quiet for a ways. Then, as we walked back on the road, between the horse show ring and the cattle barns, I told Harry, "I know what he means 'to take the bull by the horns.' One time they was a billy goat what got mean and was goin' around buttin' people. Most everone was runnin' away from it. But Uncle Sedgwick, he ran up to it just after it made a butt, grabbed the horns and twisted quick before it got itself back ready for another butt, and wrestled it down to the ground. Then Pa tied its feet real quick. Everone was scared, but Uncle Sedg, he got his courage up and did what had to be done."

We walked on quiet some more. Then as we got close to the water tower, Harry answered me.

"I've been scared of doing something about Julian's cheating, Ronson. But it's cowardly to run away from things that scare you. We have to find the courage, like your Uncle Sedgwick and that airplane pilot, to do what we have to do."

It was still warm into the evenin' and Elliedine was sittin' on the front porch. I sat beside her.

"Ellie, what do you do when you're scared of somethin'?"

"What are you scared of, Ronson?"

"No, I mean just anything. What should a body do?"

Elliedine thought for a minute, lookin' at fireflies in the field. The air was wet for a September and there was not many left to light up. There ain't nuthin' like fireflies. A flash here and gone before your eyes could focus on it. Then a flash there and then over there. It was a magic show. I watched 'em too. I loved lightnin' bugs.

"There's only one thing a body can do, Ronson. Face it and do what you have to do to make it go away."

"Sometimes it's hard to face things."

"The trouble is how big it gets. It's easy to face little things. When I chop up vegetables, I'm always a little scared I'll cut myself. But most cuts heal and the choppin' needs to be done, so I do it. It's the big things that are hard to face."

"It's easiest to put somethin' off, but it don't go away."

"Well, that's the thing, Ronson. Somethin' you're scared of is like a weed in the garden. If you leave it, it just grows bigger. It's best to pull it out fast before it can grow."

"I see what you mean, Ellie, but how do you go about facin' it?"

She thought some more.

"When a thing is too big for me—chores or schoolwork—I take it in steps. Then I think only about the first step and I do that. Then I think only about the second step and so on. A piece of it is easier to meet than the whole thing at once. And after each step, the whole thing is smaller than it was before."

Elliedine is not only the lovingist person I know and cute as a button, but she's real smart as well.

We watched the fireflies 'til it was time to go to bed.

THE NEXT DAY AT SCHOOL, I told Harry what Elliedine had said about the weed and about makin' steps.

"I think that may be true," he said. "This thing has grown a lot scarier than it was when it first happened."

"So let's break it down into steps."

"OK." He looked off without seeing for a minute. "I guess the first step is to find out who we tell about this, Julian's professor, and where he is."

"And then whatta we do?" I asked.

"Then I guess we figure out what to tell him. That is, how to tell him without getting into trouble like my dad pointed out. And step three would be doing it."

"Puttin' it into steps tells me somethin', Harry. I felt all calm when y'all spoke about steps one and two, but when y'all said three, I could hardly breathe."

"Oh, yeah, Ronson. Me, too. Just like that."

"So let's jes' look at step one now."

"I'll ask my dad. He knows most of the teachers and graduate students at the school. There are only so many."

I felt a lot better after that. I could tell Harry did, too. He started bein' cheerful instead of down in the dumps like he had been.

BUT HARRY BEIN' cheerful didn't last long. One of the courses we got to go through is called fizz ed, whatever that means. They just send us out on the field below the high school building to play softball. I think it's just for the teachers to have a hour break from puttin' up with us. They picked softball cuz there warnt no money for baseball gloves and stuff. I mean, the country's still in this depression what goes on and on and don't never end.

I do all right in the game, but Harry, he don't do so good. He gets all worried and so tense he can hardly hold the bat. When the ball comes, he has to wait 'til he can see exactly where he would connect with it and by then it's too late to swing. He always strikes out. Nobody wants him on their team.

I told him, "Harry, start yer swing as soon as the ball leaves the pitcher's hand."

He sez, "But I won't know where to swing."

I sez, "Gee, Harry, y'all can't do no worse than you're doin' now. Just try it."

Well, he does and giss what? On his second swing, he smacks the ball. It goes right between the pitcher and the first baseman, and Harry makes it to first base. He was as pleased as a rooster what had just done a hen. He almost crowed.

But then it got sour. The first baseman was two years older than Harry was and there's a big difference in both what you can do and knowin' how to do it between them two years. A lot of the country kids would be held back in grade school cuz they couldn't pass. The next year when they still couldn't pass, they'd be moved up anyway. But then they was even more behind and couldn't pass the next grade either. That made a lot of the country kids in the same grade older than the faculty kids.

He told Harry, "Don't run. If he hits the ball, don't run or I'll make you sorry." But Harry, he knew he had to run. If he didn't, he would be called out anyway. It was the game. He didn't listen.

Well, the batter hits the ball, Harry starts to run, and the first baseman sticks out a foot and trips Harry. He goes whop on the ground, face down. He hits so hard, a tooth cuts through his upper lip. He don't get up for a minute cuz he's all dazed. When he does get up, blood and dirt all over his face, the play's over and he's been touched with the ball and is out and his team loses. It was even worse than if he'd never hit the ball at all, cuz he had got their hopes up. That made everbody think even less of him than before. His eyes was all teary and his head was hangin' down and he was dizzy and hurtin'. I felt sorry for him, but nobody could do nuthin'. There wasn't no teacher out there. I guess they was all drinkin' coffee up in the school buildin'.

Another thing what riled me was grades. In grade school they done give us just Satisfactory or Unsatisfactory, but now in high school they give us letters—A, B, C, D, or F. I never did figger where E had got to. And for fizz ed, they graded us on how well we played. For most of the country kids, that was the only course they got A's and B's in instead of C's and D's. But with Harry, it was the other way around. Fizz ed was the only course he didn't get A's in. He barely got C's.

WE WALKED HOME through campus like usual. Goin' this way, from the edge of the high school ball field, well, athletic field, we'd go along College Avenue past the college liberry, which looked more like a old stone church to me—it had stain glass windows—and then go along the edge of the drill field. At the middle of the drill field, we would turn and go through the War Memorial Building, which was the athletic building, and then go across the stadium. When we got to the road, we'd be frontin' on the field where we seen Julian puttin' bugs on his corn crop. Harry's house was a little bit to the left and mine to the right. It was as short as goin' home through the town's streets and a lot more interesting cuz a lot of the time somethin' was goin' on in the stadium, like game practice.

Today when we started off, Harry was all mad and sad at the same time and wanted to say somethin' mean. So when I said somethin' about caydets, he called me down.

"Ronson, it's not said 'CAY-det.' The accent is on the second syllable and the 'a' is a short 'a.' It's said 'cah-DET.' You sound stupid when you say 'CAY-det.'"

I knowed Harry was riled and hurtin', so I went along with him. He was prob'ly right anyway. He usually was about things like that, even if he couldn't hit a ball. I started saying "cah-DET."

Well, this time, when we got to the edge of the drill field, we seen some goin'-ons with some cadets. There was two second-year fellers workin' on a rat—that's what they called the first-year fellers. They was half the drill field apart and sendin' this poor rat back and forth between 'em. We stopped for a minute to watch. We could hear what they was sayin'.

"Mister, you saw a piece of litter on the ground and didn't clean it up. Pick up that piece of paper and take it to the trash receptacle at the end of the field—on the double."

Well, he was speakin' in a Tidewater accent, so the words sounded real different from what we say here in the Blue Ridge. His "saw" was all drawn out, closer to "sa-aw-oh." His "litter" was "littah." His "ground" was said like "gra-ee-ownd." His "paper" was drawn out with no "r," like "pi-ay-pah." And like that. It was like he didn't have no r's in his talk, lessen he starts a word with one.

The rat has to run as fast as he can toward the trash can but gets stopped by the other feller. He was speakin' Tidewater, too.

"Mister, you removed a letter I had left on the grass to be collected by a colleague. That's going to cost you a demerit. You take it right back and put it where you found it—on the double." And his "letter" was "lettah" and his "right" was "raht" and stuff.

I guess it's all confusin' to folks what ain't from around here—the Virginia accents. There's Mountain in the west and Tidewater in the east where the tide come up the rivers and Piedmont in the middle and some folks can hear Shenandoah, which is north middle. People what has a good ear can even tell what part of Appalachia a body comes from.

Anyway, when the kid got back to the first cadet, he said, "Mister, you disobeyed a direct order from a superior officer. That's going to cost you two demerits. Obey the order—on the double."

See, a demerit is a punishment any upperclassman can lay on someone lower. A cadet has to pay off demerits by marchin' around the quadrangle for a hour with a heavy rifle. If a higher feller don't like the way a lower one combs his hair, he can make up stuff the lower one can't do and then pile on more demerits than he can march off. The way I look at it, it don't build nuthin' or fix nuthin' or help nobody. It just takes time the lower one could be learnin' things, which is why he's there, ain't it? It seems to me to be real dumb. If they wanted to give punishment, why couldn't they make them paint a peelin' buildin' or clean trash cans at the dining hall or somethin' that helps out?

They had that poor kid runnin' back and forth until he was red in the face and could hardly breathe and had a big pile of demerits. It was just like torture.

"Let's remember them two," I said. "So's we can skirt around if we ever come across 'em."

"OK," Harry said. "The one on the left is very light blond. If he didn't have blue eyes, I'd think he was an albino." I didn't know what that was, but right now rememberin' how he looked was on my mind. "And the one on the right has dark, wavy hair, a deep cleft in his chin, and a mole in front of his left ear."

Well, I didn't have words like that, but I sure pushed pictures of their faces down deep in my memory.

"I hope to God I don't never have any truck with those fellers," I said. We turned and went through the gym toward the stadium.

THAT NIGHT, I told Pa all about what we seen.

"Yeah, I know that goes on. It's called hazing. I heard sometimes they wake the freshmen up in the middle of the night, make them put on their full-dress uni-forms, and march them to the john. Then they order them to start pissin' and after a minute to stop. Then they march them back. If anybody's uni-form ain't perfect or if he don't start or stop on command, they give him demerits."

"Why do the folks in charge let that kind of thing go on, Pa? Don't they know what's happenin'?"

Pa nodded slowly. He was a big man, tall and strong, standin' straight. His face was what Harry called stern, but I could always see the smile lines around his eyes.

"I'm sure they do know, Ronson. They let it go on for a reason."

"Why, Pa? I don't understand."

"Let me tell you a story about when I was in the Great War."

"Yeah, Pa. I always want to hear more about that."

"Well, as you know, I mostly cared for horses in the stables. I wasn't out in the shoot-'em-up stuff much. But I seen a lot about what went on. Maybe I seen more than a lot of the gen'rals, cuz I was close and they wasn't. They always showed me writ orders, cuz I had to know what they'd been ordered to do so's I could give them enough horses and the right horses for what they needed, like to pull the big guns into place. And then I seen what happened as a result of those orders."

My eyes felt big and I didn't move or make a sound cuz I didn't want anything to stop his tellin'.

"I seen one time when they sent out a company, maybe a hunnert, hunnert fifty men, tellin' them they wanted to know where the enemy was. The colonel said to let him know if they saw any signs of the enemy. Well, the colonel knowed exactly where the enemy was. The enemy saw a small force without support movin' into their territory and they fell right on it with all they had. That was just what the colonel was waitin' for. He had his big forces around in half a circle and while the Germans was killin' off the little company, he landed on them from their sides when they wasn't lookin' and just wiped out almost a whole German regi-ment. You see?"

"I think so, Pa. It's sort of like fishin'. You put a worm on a hook and when the fish goes for the worm, you take the fish."

"That's about right, Ronson. You lose the worm, but catch the fish. And that's just fine so long as you ain't the worm."

"You mean that company they sent out was all killed?"

"Mostly. A couple of dozen men got back is all."

"Well, that was pretty shitty. Oh, I'm sorry, Pa. I didn't mean to say that."

"That's all right, boy. I know you don't talk like that lessen you're right riled."

"But what's that got to do with the hazin', Pa?"

"If you was in the company ordered to look for signs of the enemy, would you go?"

"NO! Of course not."

"Why?"

"'Cause I wouldn't want to be the worm on the hook."

"Well, that's why the hazin'. For years, they got to put up with obeyin' orders that don't make no sense. They gets to the place where they obey any order, makin' sense or not. That's what the gen'rals and colonels have to have. Troops that do what they're told without tryin' to make sense of it."

"I guess I can see that, Pa, but I don't like it. But

some of the upper folks is just plain cruel to the lower folks. Ain't there some limit to how hurtful they get?"

"I'm afraid, Ronson, they have to learn that, too. Most times, you get a colonel what's got good sense. But sometimes, you get a mean one, and you gotta obey him just like the good ones. In this world, some folks is just plain mean."

The sun was goin' down real fast. When it's the longest days or the shortest days, the sun seems to move real slow, but when the day lasts the same time as the night, it goes so fast. Tonight, I watched the sun shootin' down. Everthing was all warm and green and growin' when there was lots of sun. That must mean the sun is good and life is good when God gives us lots of sun, but it can get purty poor when he don't. Or, mebbe, the sun is God. *Oh, Lordy, bite yer tongue. Ye done thought what you ain't supposed to think. God's gonna get ye.* Unless God's the sun. Then he'll just shine on ye. *Oh, my, oh, my, I done it agin.*

"I'm done sorry, God," I said out loud. "But you must have made the sun, mustn't you?"

I had a hard time goin' to sleep that night. I was tuckered enough, but my mind kept thinkin' about those two peckerwoods from the flatlands down east. And why God let them do what they did. I guessed I was growin' up, and I didn't think I liked it.

4

OCTOBER 1939

Autumn in Blacksburg always made folks feel good. I didn't know if I liked spring or fall better. The breeze was pickin' up and had a right smart feel to it. The leaves was all purty and the squirrels and boomers was goin' wild, runnin' back and forth and up and down trees, gettin' in their nuts for the winter. You could start to feel cold in the shade of a tree, but still felt warm when you got out into Mister Sun. It was Saturday mornin' and no school. I went over to see Harry.

Jes' as I was gettin' there, Harry came runnin' up the black cinder driveway between the laurel bushes, yellin' at me.

"Ronson! Ronson! The garbage wagon's coming."

I turned to look and, sure enough, there came the horses clop-cloppin' along, with the metal rims on the wagon wheels grindin' along on the concrete of the road. The garbage man, Mister Sarver, was lumped down on his seat, holdin' the reins, although he didn't have to. The horses knowed the way to go better'n he did. He was along just to dump the cans into the back on the smelly mess and stir the flies up into a cloud. There was so many flies, I didn't know how they all got out of the way when he dumped. Or maybe they didn't all. Nobody could tell.

Mister Sarver didn't say much, no more'n he had do. He was old and all wrinkled and his skin looked like the leather bag Harry's pa carried back and forth to his office. He didn't have but two or three teeth left and his hair looked like a rain cloud —all gray and blowin' this way and that. If no grownups was around, he'd go in the corner of the garage to take a leak. It made Doctor Hillson awful mad, but he couldn't never catch Mister Sarver doin' it.

Well, we just put up with the smell from the wagon. It was just there and we never thought about it. What intersted us was the horses. We'd squirrel away a piece of apple or somethin' to feed them and we'd pet 'em and hug 'em. But best of all, Mister Sarver would let us climb up on the seat and hold the reins and drive the horses from the road down to the house and back. We'd slap the reins up and down on the horses' backs and go "chuck chuck" and stuff. Of course, the horses never paid us no mind no matter what we did.

Goin' back out, when we got to the road, Mister Sarver would take the reins and stop the horses and we knowed to get down. He didn't say nuthin', so neither did we. But, lookin' back on it, I think he was glad of the company, but jes' too beat down to talk. He'd clop-clop and rumble off, and we'd feel sad we wouldn't see the horses agin 'til next week.

I turned to Harry and asked him if he'd talked to his pa about Julian.

"No, Ronson. Dad's been working late on some research project and stays busy grading papers when he gets home. I haven't had a chance."

"You sure you ain't been puttin' it off?"

"Nooo," he sez, drawin' the word out. "But he's home now. Let's go ask him."

Doctor Hillson was sittin' on his bed, holdin' a red pencil with a pile of papers in his lap. I wondered why he didn't do it at their big eatin' table. He could have a whole big side to hisself.

"Good morning, Ronson. What are you up to today?" he said with a smile. He was formal-like, but I could tell he liked kids. He always listened to me like I had somethin' important to say.

"Just fine, Doctor Hillson, sir," I said as po-lite as I could be. But then I saw I didn't answer what he asked me, and I could feel my face gettin' red and I shut way up.

"Dad," Harry said. "A while ago you said we should go and tell about that student we saw releasing worms on the corn. But we don't know who to go to."

"Harry, you should have done that last month. You're well aware that the corn has been harvested. All the evidence is gone. It will be your word against his now."

"Oh, gosh," Harry said, suddenly all worried like.

"But I think you should still do it. It's not like you have any motive. And, if he has been biasing the data, he would have motive to deny it. Therefore, you are more likely to be believed."

"Oh," Harry said. I didn't think that was much of a answer.

"You want to know which professor to go and see. To know that, we need to know who the student was."

"I know that much," Harry said. "It was Julian Martin."

"Oh, yes. I know who he is. I had him in organic chemistry. He seemed to be a bright boy. His advisor is Professor Fox. He's officed in the agricultural building."

He stood up, went to his leather case, and pulled out some kind of list and a pad of paper.

"Here. I'll write down his floor and office number."

He handed the sheet to Harry. "Now there's one thing you need to be very, very careful about. You don't want to look like you're accusing Julian of anything. If you do, and it turns out his actions were legitimate, then you will be guilty of falsely accusing him. You could get into trouble. So this is what you want to do. Stay strictly with what you actually saw, nothing more. Do not draw any conclusions about it. Let Professor Fox draw the conclusions. Do you understand that?"

"I think so, Dad. I'm to say just that we saw him spreading the worms and didn't know why, so we thought we should tell about it in case it was important."

"Exactly, Harry. You do not—*not*—use the word 'cheat' or anything like it. Do you understand, Ronson?"

"Yessir," I said. "We say just what we seen, not what we think."

"That's it. That way you do the job without the risk of getting into any trouble."

Then he sat back down on his bed and picked up his pile of papers. We could see he wanted to get back to work.

"Thanks, Dad," Harry said, and we went out.

On Monday, Harry and I was talkin' while we was walkin' home from school.

"Well, Ronson, we know who to go to and where to find him. Now we have to figure out what to tell him."

"I guess we just say it. We seen Julian puttin' worms on some of the corn."

"But then he would say, 'Why are you telling me about this?'" Harry scratched his head with one finger, then went on. "And we can't say why, like my dad told me, because we would be accusing Julian of wrongdoing when we don't really know if he did. So we couldn't answer him. And if we couldn't tell him why we were telling him, he would tell us just to go and mind our own business."

"Couldn't we say 'Cuz he might be doin' somethin' wrong'? We're not sayin' he did. We're just sayin' 'might.'"

"I don't know. But my dad was very insistent that we not say anything except what we saw."

"Well, shucks, Harry. We's stuck off in a corner agin. We can't say it, but it ain't no use in goin' unless we can say it."

Harry hung his head agin. He did that too much. I hope he don't grow up doin' that. He won't amount to a hill of beans if he keeps doin' that. He needs to hold his head up, even when things go bad, like my pa does.

We didn't say no more, cuz neither of us knowed what to say. We just walked on.

Then, just as we was leavin' the gym and goin' up the steps to the athletic field, we come across Elliedine comin' down.

"Hi, Ellie," I sez. "Where ye goin'?"

Elliedine smiled that smile what would melt a block of ice as big as we used in the ice boxes to keep our food cool.

"Hi, Ronson. Hi, Harry. I'm goin' to the college liberry. I got to look up some stuff for a history class."

They let us go there, cuz my pa worked for the college.

"What period of history is your class about?" asked Harry. Only Harry would think to ask somethin' like that.

"It's American history, about how we was fightin' the British to get free."

"One hundred sixty years ago," Harry said. How'd he know that? I'll never figger Harry.

By then we was up to the field and she was goin' in the door, so we quit talkin'.

"What does anybody care about times so long back, Harry? It don't matter to us now."

"On the contrary," Harry said. I think he meant I was wrong. "It matters every day. That's why we're free instead of a colony like India or South Africa. Or even Canada."

I tell you! Harry has the craziest ideas. Is my pa more free than a pa in Canada? They both has to work or their famblies will go hungry.

Anyway, by then we was above the stadium to the road and had to split up to go home.

TOWARD SUPPER TIME, Elliedine come home. One look at her and I knowed somethin' was wrong. She didn't glow like she had a little piece of Mister Sun inside. She just walked in with her head down and went up to the bedroom. Pa and Uncle Sedg was still at work, but Ma saw it. Ma follered her up. I wanted to know what was goin' on, so I picked up a schoolbook and sat on a step at the bottom of the stairs, tryin' to look like I was studyin'. I could just hear some of the words she was sayin' to Ma.

After a couple minutes, Elliedine began to cry. I hadn't heard her cry for a long spell. Somethin' was really wrong. Ma kept talkin' to her in a low sweet voice. I couldn't hear what she was sayin', but I think she was tryin' to get Ellie to come out with it. Finally, Ellie sort of screamed and started talkin' loud like if the Claytor Lake Dam had broke.

"They done me, Ma. Them awful caydets done me."

Ma asked somethin' quiet and Elliedine answered. I couldn't hear and moved up a couple of steps. I figured long as they was talkin' back and forth, they wouldn't come down. But just in case, I set some paper on the open book and held a pencil ready, scowlin' like I was thinkin' hard. I could hear Elliedine.

"I was walkin' through the gym to go to the liberry and these two caydets stopped me and started sweet-talkin' to me. I wouldn't pay them no heed nor even look at them, so they done grab me and tuck me up the stairs. I tried to get loose, but there was two of them and they're bigger'n me and I couldn't. They took me into the room where they keep all the spare uniforms and put a overcoat on the floor and pushed me down."

She started to cry agin. Ma talked agin, so quiet I couldn't make out what she was sayin'. Then Ellie come out louder agin, between breathin' real hard.

"They hurt me, Ma. They hurt me. Both of 'em did it. And when they got finished and buttoned up they just stood there for a minute lookin' down at me. I was cryin' and cryin'. And they laughed at me. They just laughed at me, Ma. They laughed and laughed. And then they went out."

Ma talked quiet agin. When Elliedine spoke next, she was quieter, but I could still make out what she was sayin'.

"I just lay there for a spell tryin' to figger what

to do, but I couldn't figger anything, so I just come home. Oh, Ma. Oh, Ma."

And then they both talked quiet. I couldn't hear no more and I didn't want Ma to know I heard it, so I put the book back and went out into the field. The sky didn't seem so bright no more. I done feel something mean and ugly buildin' inside. It was a feelin' I didn't never have before. I couldn't hear a single bird singin'. I started kickin' clods of dirt and I kicked 'em and kicked 'em.

"They is goin' to pay," I said to myself out loud. "I'm goin' to get them two fellers. They done cut down Elliedine's…well, I can't find a word for it. Maybe 'spirit'? 'Soul'? They ain't the right words, but I reckon 'soul' will have to do. They done cut down Ellie's soul like a threshin' machine cuts down wheat."

I looked up at the sky. There was some dark clouds like it was fixin' to rain.

"I vow," I said to the dark clouds. I admit I ain't all that good at vowin' to God in church. I say the words, but they don't mean much. They is just words. But now I was vowin' with all my heart.

"I vow I'm goin' to get even with those fellers. Sooner or later. Somehow. I vow I'm gonna," I told the clouds. And they started cryin' rain like they done heard me.

In the next days, Elliedine done her chores and went to school, but she done been turned off. Her spirit had just gone away like a when a light bulb burns out. I tried a couple times to hold her hand to make her feel better, but she didn't want nobody to touch her, not even me.

I didn't go to see Harry. I sat home and done my homework. I hated homework, but it seemed better'n thinkin' about Ellie. Seemed like doin' somethin' miserable was right. Elliedine was miserable and if I was just a little bit miserable, maybe I was sharin' miserable with Elliedine. Well, I can't explain it, but that's what I done.

After a few days, Harry come over to my house. He didn't come there much, I think cuz he didn't feel right at my place. He could talk to p'fessors and men what owned businesses in town and folks like that real easy, but he had a hard time talkin' to Pa or Ma. He didn't know what to say or how to say it.

Anyway, he come around.

"You haven't come over for days and days, Ronson," he said. "What's going on? Are you angry with me for something?"

"No, Harry, I ain't," I said.

I walked out into the field and he followed. I kicked some more dirt clods. I been kickin' dirt clods every day. I was surprised they was any clods left, but I guess it was a big field.

"Harry, don't tell nobody about this, but Elliedine done been hurt. Some cadets hurt her."

"Hurt her? How?"

"Well, you seen a male animal go after a female when she's in heat? We seen bulls and stallions and dogs and roosters do it."

"Yes, my mom read me a book about that when I was smaller. It impregnates the female with sperm and starts babies."

"Your ma? My ma and pa ain't never said nuthin' about that to me. I just seen it in the barns and fields and chicken coops. If the female's in heat, she puts up with it, almost wants it, but with chickens the rooster pecks the hen on the back of the neck and holds her down while he jumps on her. She don't like it much."

"Why are you talking about this, Ronson?"

"Cuz that's what they done to Elliedine, Harry. They done hold her down like a rooster does a hen and jump on her. They hurt her. And she ain't the same. You know how some men break a horse by beatin' it 'til it give up? My pa tames a horse by showin' it love 'til it wants to share. Pa sez that's what a marriage should be. But these fellers, they done hurt Ellie 'til they broke her. And you can't never tell nobody I told you about it."

"What are your folks going to do about it?"

"They's awful mad. Uncle Sedg wanted to go

beat them up and hang them on a meat hook. But Pa, he sez they ain't nuthin' we kin do. He sez we's the poor and poor folks don't have no power. He sez if he beats them or kills them, the rich folks will put him in jail cuz they got fancy lawyers and then nobody can take care of our fambly. He sez if we complain to the law, they'll deny it and get Pa fired and if he was fired, that keeps him from getting another job and the fambly's in trouble just as bad."

Harry stared at a blue mountain in the distance for a bit. Then he sez, "Couldn't your dad write an anonymous letter to the school authorities telling them what happened? I'm sure they'd investigate it."

"A what letter?"

"Anonymous. Unsigned and written so nobody will know who wrote it."

I rolled my eyes while shakin' my head. That Harry! "I don't know if Pa knows how to write a letter. I never seen him do it. He don't think that way."

"Then we could write one. Block letters so they couldn't trace the handwriting, like I read in an Ellery Queen story."

"We'd have to name Ellie. Then they'd start lookin' at the fambly. Pa sez he'd lose his job and we wouldn't have a house to live in or anything to eat."

"But it happened to Ellie. Wouldn't that tip the scales?"

"No, Harry. We got no proof. It would be Elliedine's word, a kid's word, against two rich grownups."

"That's awful, Ronson. Just awful. Elliedine is such a sweetheart. Everybody says so, even grownups."

"She ain't no more. They done took that away from her."

AFTER THAT, since Harry knew about it anyway, I started goin' over to his house agin. We talked about it. Harry, he said we gotta find a way to get back at them.

"I tell you what, Ronson," he said, all riled. "We'll find out where they live down in the Tidewater and go put a bomb in their house."

"That'd hurt their folks and not them. They'd still be up here at the school."

"We'll wait until a school break and then do it."

"You don't know how to make a bomb, Harry."

"I'll find out. I'll go to the library and read up on it."

"Yeah, Harry, let's go find that book called 'How to make a bomb big enough to blow up a house but small enough to hide in your pocket while you take a bus to Tidewater and pay for it all with money you ain't got.'"

"Oh, Ronson, you're exaggerating just to make it sound impossible."

"Mebbe so, Harry, but where're you goin' to get the money to buy the stuff what goes into a bomb?"

"Well, then, what are *you* going to do, smart alec?"

"I'm gonna take our Louisville Slugger baseball bat and beat their brains out."

See, in baseball season, Harry and I got to be batboys cuz we was always around cuz we live so close. The school has the highest quality bats and balls you can buy. We line the bats all up by length and weight. We know what bat each batter wants for his size and strength and have it ready when he gets up to bat. Some wants light bats they got more control over. Others want heavier bats that don't get hits so often but drive the ball farther when they do get hits. And like that. Anyway, once in a while the pitcher throws the ball real hard and the batter hits it real hard and it makes a crack in the bat. Then they'll give it to us cuz it ain't no more good to them. We put a screw or two in to hold the crack—kids can't hit hard enough for the crack to matter—and we got a bat better than any other boy's pa will buy him. All the boys in the neighborhood get together on a Saturday and play ball in Mac Holdaway's big front yard. Harry kin hit pretty good when it's just us, even though he always strikes out when the country kids is all yellin' at him in the schoolyard. So that's what I was talkin' about with our Louisville Slugger bat.

"Oh, yeah, Ronson. I can see it now. You walk up to two grown men carrying your bat and whack them both while they just stand there at attention waiting for it and nobody sees you do it and you walk away. Good for you."

I have to say Harry was right. It wasn't as crazy as a bomb, but I could see it wouldn't work.

Harry went on. "We don't even know who they are. Are you going to whack the entire cadet corps to be sure you get the right ones?"

"Oh, shut up, Harry," I said.

"You know, Ronson, we didn't think about it before, but the first thing we have to do is find out who they are. We can't do anything until we do that."

I was stopped cold. I just sat there. I was so dumb. Of course we have to find out who they are.

"Why don't you ask Elliedine?" Harry said.

"She won't talk about it. Fact is, she don't talk to me at all no more. She just sits and won't talk and won't look at anybody. We used to talk all the time. Now she just goes away if I try to talk to her."

"Did she tell your mom who they are?" asked Harry.

"Ma don't know I know," I said. "I don't think

she knows who they are and I don't want to upset her any more by askin' her and lettin' on I know all about it."

We just stood there, thinkin' and thinkin' and gettin' nuthin' thought. And there the situation sat, side by side with Julian's fertilizer cheat, for all the world like they both had been forgot.

5
NOVEMBER 1939

One day after school, Harry and I was sittin' in our blowed-over tree. Harry made out like it was a rocket ship, right out of "Buck Rogers in the 25th Century." Buck Rogers is one of the best stories in the funny papers. He goes into space in rocket ships what is all streamlined with pointy noses so the air out in space don't slow them down. Harry and I even got little goggles, fur-lined for the cold around the edges, like they show folks in space wearin'. I guess it must be to keep the wind out of their eyes cuz they're in open cockpits out there in space. Harry and I love the funnies.

Harry's pa reads the funnies with him every day. That's real nice. I know my pa loves me, but he wouldn't never, ever read funnies with me. Fact, I never seen him read, 'cept orders on what farmin' he got to do. Once or twice I was over at the Hillsons' when it was funnies time and Doctor Hillson let me sit on the other side of him from Harry, sit real close almost like I cuddled with my ma when I was little. It felt good. I was just warm and all safe. He read "Mutt and Jeff" and "Major Hoople." Then when he come to "Joe Palooka" and "Little Orphan Annie," he said we should all read parts like in a play. I didn't read too good and got all embarrassed, so he said I could be Annie's dog Sandy. He read Daddy Warbucks, Harry read Annie, and whenever Sandy's turn come, I said "Wuuf!" Well, I never had so much fun! It made the pitchers come alive, bein' part of it. I could jes' see Annie steppin' right out of the page like she could see where she was goin'. Harry got all bothered cuz she didn't have no pupils in her eyes, but I didn't pay it no heed.

Well, to get back to our spaceship tree, Harry wanted to play like we was Buck Rogers and his sidekick Doctor Huer fightin' Killer Kane.

"Ain't we gettin' a li'l grown up for that stuff, Harry?" I said.

But Harry was into it. He pulled a branch to fire our ray guns. "There he goes," he snickered. "We've riddled his spaceship full of holes."

I sighed but went along. "Yeah," I said, "I guess he's going down now for sure."

Harry cheered, but then looked a little funny.

"Where's down?" he asked. "We're in space."

"What do you mean, where's down?" I said. "Down is down, thataway." I pointed down.

"But that's toward the center of the Earth, being pulled by gravity," Harry said. "Are you saying that Killer's ship is being pulled from outer space all the way back to crash on Earth?"

"Well, where in the love of God do you think it'll fall to?" I said, a little louder than I should.

"More like succumbing to the gravitational pull of the nearest heavenly body. Maybe it's pulled into a star and burns up."

I didn't say no more. Sometimes folks got so much edication they can't imagine things. I know Harry did. It wasn't no fun no more. I just started to climb down.

"Aw, Ronson, I didn't mean it. Don't go."

"Let's do somethin' else," I said.

We walked around the yard for a couple minutes, endin' up at the sandpile. We looked at it and tried to think if we wanted to make a racetrack for cars or a fort, but just lookin' at it made me want to kick the sand around and walk off.

Sometimes grown-up ways of seein' things sneaks into kids' doin's. The fun just shrivels up and goes away like a water drop in a hot skillet. It looks like grownups don't never have no fun. I was thinkin' I didn't never want to grow up.

Harry was hangin' his head agin like he does

when he feels he done somethin' wrong. I think he didn't want to grow up neither.

"Well, Harry," I said, kind of mean like. "Mebbe we should get serious. Mebbe we should go over to see P'fessor Fox and get this Julian business over with."

I expected him to say no and get us to playin' agin, but he surprised me.

"You're right," he said. "Let's get it over with."

And so we started walkin' over toward the aggie building.

Harry pulled the piece of paper his pa had give him back a while ago. It was all crinkled up and dirty. Dirt and lint and a little sand fell out when he unfolded it. But he could still read it. He read the office number and we walked up and down the hallways 'til we come on it. P'fessor Fox was inside, sittin' at his desk. I wondered what in the wide world a body could do all day just sittin' there. Harry knocked, even though the door was wide open.

"Come in," the p'fessor said, turnin' and lookin' at us. I could see he was surprised to see two boys come to his office. "What can I do for you gentlemen?"

Well, didn't nobody ever call me a gentleman

before. I didn't know if I liked it or not. On the one hand, it felt good, but on the other, I was scared he was makin' fun of us. But I just kept my trap shut.

Harry did the talkin'. He didn't seem scared to talk to high-up folks.

"Sir," he said, "there is an issue we'd like to bring to your attention."

Harry must have figgered out what we was goin' to say before he got there. I wouldn't have been able to say boo, myself. And he knowed to say "sir." I don't think I would have remembered to say that.

We've heard high-class folks say that any southern gentleman always sez "sir" to another southern gentleman, whether above him or below him. When you say "southern gentleman," you have a whole bunch of meaning that damnyankees don't get at all. Unless of course you're referrin' to the whiskey by that name. I've heard that southern p'fessors call their students "sir," cuz they assume that anybody going to college has got to be a gentleman.

Anyway, P'fessor Fox, he said, "First, why don't you tell me who you are?"

So Harry tells him who he is and who I am and then goes on.

"Last August, we observed something we thought strange, so we thought it only right to let you know about it. We found out that it occurred in a crop of corn being raised by your student, Julian Martin, so we came to you."

"And what did you observe, Mr. Hillson?"

He done call Harry "Mister Hillson"! I realized my mouth had fell open and I popped it closed agin. But these college folks, they's all a lot more formal than ordinary folks. Else mebbe they's playin' by a different set of rules.

"Well...." Harry hesitated. He started lookin' scared. He was pullin' hisself together, I could see. The p'fessor, he just waited, all patient like.

"Last August, Ronson and I were walking through the cornfield across from the Miles Stadium entrance. His house is north of the field and mine is south, so we often cut across the field when we go back and forth." He didn't bother to say we was cuttin' the corn silk into rabbit tobacco. "We saw Julian in the field and he was spreading little worms all over the growing corn ears. We thought it was strange."

"So you suspected there was chicanery afoot," added the p'fessor.

I begin to get lost in their big words.

"I'm not accusing anybody of anything," Harry said, real quick.

"I understand that. You would just like to have the incident explained to ease your minds."

"Yes, sir," said Harry. "That's about it."

"Well, I won't ask why you waited so long to tell me. I can see this is hard for you."

He looked out the window for a minute, then turned back to us.

"Tell you what. Why don't I get Julian to explain it to you. He's just down the hall."

I tensed all up, ready to run out. That's what I wanted to do. I could see that Harry was all nervous, kind of sputterin', but he didn't have any idea what he could say. P'fessor Fox got up, walked to the door, leaned out, and called in a loud voice, "Julian, would step in here for a moment please?" Then he came back and sat down.

In two shakes of a lamb's tail Julian scuttled in. He stopped dead when we saw us and started lookin' confused.

"These two young gentlemen saw you spreading infestation on your corn crop before the harvest. Perhaps you would explain to them what you were doing?"

Julian looked like he couldn't decide whether to be mad or flattered. But I don't suppose he could do anything but what his boss told him, so he started talkin'.

"I was comparing the effectiveness of a formulation of fertilizer. I needed an equal number of randomly positioned fields of crops being raised in each of two groups: with fertilizer and without. I had three types of crop, corn, wheat, and soy, so I had a two-way experiment. I went to Dr. Boyd Harshbarger in the Mathematics Department—he's a statistician—for the design. He said that by using a two-way analysis of variance—that's a pretty new form of analysis—I could tell if there was a fertilizer effect across all crops, if there was a crop difference regardless of fertilizer, and if there was a fertilizer effect different for one type of crop from another."

He paused and looked at us. To me, he might as well have been talking in the language the men on the moon use. I don't think Harry understood it all, but he must have gotten some of it, cuz he nodded his head a time or two.

Julian looked at his p'fessor, who nodded. He went on.

"Then my thesis committee wanted to know if the fertilizer reduced or facilitated the effect of infestation. I went back to Dr. Harshbarger and he proposed a balanced three-way design, where I could add in the effect of infestation. To have that, I had to infest a randomly chosen half of the fields of each crop and of fertilizer or not. That's what I was doing."

Julian shut up then, trying not to look angry or satisfied with hisself, or whatever he was feelin'. The p'fessor turned to look at us, smiled a little smile, and waited.

So, while I didn't get the way they was settin'

the exper'ment up, it looked like he was spreadin' his worms all legal like and P'fessor Fox knew all about it. I started to turn to go out when Harry spoke up. It was clear to me that Harry hadn't thought and was just blurtin' things out.

"But you were looking back and forth like you didn't want to be seen."

Julian was getting riled now. He turned a little red and started talkin' louder than before.

"I was looking around to estimate the number of stalks of corn I had to infest. I had to place the worms approximately equally throughout the field. I was asking myself if I had enough worms to finish the infestation." He was gettin' madder and madder.

P'fessor Fox turned to Julian and said, "That was a nice summary, Julian. Thank you so much for the explanation."

Julian turned and stalked out.

P'fessor Fox, he turns to us and said, "Thank you, gentlemen, for coming forward. I assume it was motivated by your integrity in trying to see that science is done honestly."

Harry nodded. I just stared at the p'fessor, tryin' to figger out whatall he just said. He went on.

"You can see that the infestation was planned and part of the experiment. That should end your concern. And I thank you for that concern. Look, you boys did a good thing. I hope you have learned from this that it's never wrong to pursue good ethics. Your inquiring minds can now be at peace." He gave a great big smile like he was real pleased with his fancy words. We could see there was nuthin' more to say.

"Yes, thank you, sir," Harry said and turned to go.

I can't tell y'all how glad I was to get out of there.

WALKING BACK HOME, I said, "I didn't get none of all that gobbledegook. Did you?"

"A little," Harry said. "But I got the important thing. It was all part of a plan and there was no chicanery about it."

There was that word agin.

"Chicory, Harry? We make a crappy-tastin' coffee from the roots when we don't have enough money for real coffee."

"Not chicory, Ronson, chicanery. It means cheating."

"Then why in God's name don't ye just SAY cheatin'?" I said, feelin' all stormy.

Harry just sighed a big sigh but didn't say nuthin' more.

When I got home, Pa and Uncle Sedgwick was on the front porch sittin' up real straight in their chairs 'stead of lollin' down like usual. They was goin' at each other, all riled up over politics.

"Mr. Roosevelt is doin' more for poor folks than any president ever done, Mason," Uncle Sedg said to my pa. "The guv'mint can't just wave a magic wand and make everbody have enough. Takes time."

"Yeah, well. I guess he's helpin' some poor folks, but at the cost of hurtin' others," Pa said. "His Mr. Wallace, he's payin' folks not to plant crops and to kill pigs and like that. It wastes food and makes prices high for folks what don't got no money."

"So you gonna vote for somebody like Mr. Herbert Hoover or Mr. Alf Landon what don't help any poor at all?"

"I didn't say that, Sedgwick. It's a year 'til the next election, and I'll see who runs and what they say. Them dumb folks over in Europe done got theyselves in a war agin—and you and I know first-hand what that was like last time. I gotta see which candidate is gonna keep us out of it."

Uncle Sedg quieted down. He looked like he was thinkin' deep.

"I gotta agree with you there, Mason. I don't want to go back to that. I guess we'll just wait a spell and see." He settled down droopin' over his chair, lookin' for all the world like the rag doll Elliedine had when she was little.

"Pa," I said, "what was that about killin' pigs? And payin' people for not doin' stuff?"

"Well, Ronson, Mr. Roosevelt sez that the more food we raise, the less it costs, so the less farmers get. He wants to limit the amount of food we raise to keep prices high enough for farmers to make a livin'. To do that, his Mr. Wallace, his man for agriculture, made rules that you gotta kill off the animals more'n you're allowed to have and you can't plant more'n so many acres of crops. He's even payin' some farmers to not plant at all."

"But, Pa, if he keeps prices high, that hurts us, don't it? We can't buy hardly enough food as it is."

"That's the way I see it, Ronson. It seems to me that if I was to get less money for each bushel but raise more bushels, I'll get the same amount of money at the end and there'd be more food that costs less to the poor."

"Then what's Uncle Sedg fussin' about?"

"Sedgwick don't see it that way. He sez we gotta do somethin' about this dang de-pression and Mr. Wallace's rules will make the economy better in the long run if'n we just hold on long enough."

"But how long's that, Pa? It's been a de-pression for years and everbody's hungry. It ain't right to kill pigs when everbody's hungry."

"That's why I'm so mad, Ronson. It ain't right.

He sez if there's fewer pigs, the prices go higher and the pig farmers can make a livin'. Maybe that makes more money for pig farmers, but it makes pork cost more so's anyone who's not a pig farmer has to pay more money, which they ain't got. So how does that help folks? There is more folks what ain't pig farmers than folks what is, so I say he's makin' the de-pression worse."

"It jes' don't seem right, Pa. And supposin' a farmer don't agree to kill his pigs. They gonna put him in jail?"

"I don't know what they'd do, Ronson," he said, shakin' his head side to side real slow. "I just don't know. But one thing I do know is that Mr. Roosevelt is from New York. He's a damnyankee, and damnyankees from big cities up North always wants to hurts poor folks in the South. It's been like that ever since the War Between the States. I remember hearin' my grandpa tellin' what it was like after that war. In the war, the North destroyed all the cattle and crops the South had and left everbody poor. Some folks even starved to death. Then they pass a law what sez any man what fought for the South couldn't vote—and by the end of the war, everbody 'cept little boys and old men had been called up for the army. So local people pretty much couldn't vote. That left them what come down from the North as the only ones who could make laws. So they raised taxes. Southern folks with land but no cattle and no crops and nobody to work the land couldn't pay the big taxes, so the northerners took their land for tax payments. It made everbody in the South poor and hungry and cold. And took away their future while they was at it. And they keep doin' things like that to this day, findin' ways to suck money out of the South and keep it down. That's why we don't trust nobody from up North."

"That's awful, Pa."

"I thought it might be different now with Cactus Jack Garner as vice president—he's from Uvalde, Texas—but I guess the vice one don't have much power compared to the big one."

"You mean that's why we're poor, Pa?"

"Well, not directly. It's sort of like a dam what makes a lake. If'n you drain water out the dam, the water upstream from the dam ain't the water drainin' out, but the whole lake goes down."

"Like maybe ...." I had to think on that for a minute. "Like if they make folks down in Richmond poor, they couldn't buy as much coal and that make our miners up here more poor?"

"Like that, Ronson, like that. But they sure don't care. My own grandpa told me about kids so hungry their ribs was stickin' out when the damnyankees come in and raised taxes and took their land and made things worse."

"Must be still goin' on, Pa. There's a boy, Archie,

in school—his pa mines up Coal Bank Holler way —what don't have two shoes. He wears one tennis shoe and one leather shoe what they found in the trash. Oh, yeah, and there's the Ellett boys. Brothers. They got only one set of clothes 'twixt them. One comes to school one day and t'other the next day."

Pa nodded. He done take what I said serious. He's a good pa that way. Some pa's don't listen to nuthin' their chilluns say. I felt good we was talkin' back and forth 'stead of jes' me listenin'.

"It's bad, Ronson. I don't know when it's goin' to end."

"Some of them don't have nuthin' to eat at lunch at school. Ma gives me a piece of bread I keep in my pocket, but Harry's ma makes him a lunch he carries in a bag. It's two pieces of bread with peanut butter between them and he has a banana. I seen Archie ask him for the peels he pulls off the banana. Archie scrapes the inside of the peel on his teeth and gets a little bit of white stuff."

We sat for a spell, quiet. Uncle Sedgwick had been listenin' to it all and after we was all finished, he spoke up.

"And on top of it all …," I could hear bitter in his voice, "we might have a war comin'. Mr. Roosevelt sez he don't want a war, but he's buildin' up the army and buildin' ships for the navy, although I don't know where he gets the money when the whole country is poor."

Pa's face turned all gray. He looked so sad it made me want to cry.

"They could kill me before I'd go back to that. And I don't want my boy to go to that."

"A-men," Uncle Sedgwick said.

"What was it like, Pa?" I asked.

Uncle Sedgwick answered for him. "We don't even want you to know, Ronson. It was misery day to day, and then came a fight with fear and pain and death all around. Mothers spend their lives raisin' boys and makin' 'em into good men, and then with one cannon shell a dozen of them mothers got nuthin' left but a memory. War is just the worst hell ever was."

Pa added in, "Y'all's a smart boy, Ronson. Y'all asks good questions. I know we's poor and can't hope for you to be all edicated and do more'n a workin' job in life, but, I swear to God, it's better'n your gettin' blowed up in some mud field. I won't have it. I won't."

"Soup's on," Ma called from inside.

"What we got tonight?" Pa called back.

Ma came to the door.

"I said 'soup,' didn't I? And if'n I hear one complaint, that feller gets a short bowl."

∽

Dinner was quiet. These days it always was, cuz Elliedine didn't say a word and didn't nobody feel they could make a joke or even talk 'bout normal things cuz it might make Ellie feel like we wasn't all hurtin' for her. I 'spect the quiet hurt her just as much, cuz she knowed why we was quiet. Well, we're damned if we do and damned if we don't. There wasn't no subject we could talk about and so we had to keep quiet. We all ate quick and went off to find somethin' else to do. That was hard in so small a house in wintertime. I went outside.

I put on my sweater what my grandma done knit me before she died and my jacket on top of that. It didn't keep me warm, but it slowed the cold down so's I could stay outside for quite a spell. I was lookin' up at the moon, thinkin' how it gets colder on nights that ye can see it. Ain't no clouds to hold in the heat what's comin' out the ground.

Elliedine come out. I think she was goin' to stand there like I was, but seen I was already doin' it. She shuffled around and started to walk off.

"Ellie," I said. She jumped. She jumps every time they's a noise, a door slams, or a car backfires out on the road. Once I even seen her jump when Ma shut the Bible with a little slap.

"Ellie, talk to me. I know what happent. It's eatin' you up. Talk to me."

She looked so sad.

"Talkin' ain't gonna help, Ronson. I can't undo it."

Hearin' the way she said it was like a knife cuttin' me. This wasn't my Elliedine where every word showed the fun of livin'. This was a ol' woman, worn down by the meanness in the world. I couldn't stand it.

I stepped close to her, puttin' my arm around her shoulders. She flinched like I was goin' to hurt her. Then, finally, she melted and put her face on my shoulder.

"I'm so alone, Ronson. Pa sez I can't say nuthin' cuz people'll look down on me even though it wasn't my fault. He sez it would bring shame to our fambly."

"No, Ellie. Nobody what ain't gone through it got any right to tell you that. Pa don't know what he's talkin' about. He ain't never had nuthin' like that happen to him, so he don't know."

"Ronson, has you tol' anybody?"

Oh, Lordy, Lordy. What was I gonna say? I didn't want to lie, both cuz it was my sister who always told the truth and cuz Ma sez lyin' is wrong. But I couldn't bring myself to hurt her any more. I sort of cut it down the middle—half of it truth and half of it lie.

"Well, Elliedine, Harry can see somethin's wrong, but he don't know the whole truth."

She looked at me with the saddest eyes I ever

seen. Her eyes seemed to sink back in her head like they didn't want to see what they was seein'.

"Don't lie to me, Ronson. You ain't never lied to me before. Never. If Harry just thought we was havin' a fambly squabble or somethin', you wouldn't have said his name."

I swallered hard. I could've hit myself upside the head. I done real bad. I hurt Elliedine more, I done what I'd promised Ma I'd never do, and I made myself into what the preacher calls a sinner, all in one sentence. I looked down at the ground.

"Shame on me, Ellie. Shame on me. I done you wrong. Yeah, Harry knows, but he ain't never told nobody. He just feels bad for ye like I do."

Elliedine done heave a sigh so big it reminded me of Mother Nature sighin' in a winter storm.

"Ronson," Elliedine said, "we got a light between us what other folks ain't got. Don't never snuff it out with a lie."

"I tell ye one thing, Ellie. Somehow, some way, I'm gonna get them peckerwoods. I swear I'm gonna."

Elliedine's mouth smiled her old sweet smile, but her eyes stayed sunk. I could see she didn't believe it.

"Thank you, Ronson. You're a good brother."

6

DECEMBER 1939

In December, it gets real airish out. It's gettin' colder by the day and we's all jammed up in our little house like chickens in their coop. Five people in three rooms. Well, I admit Pa and Uncle Sedg go out and work in the day and Elliedine and I go to school. It's just evenin' that's all jammed up. And weekends. We looks forward to weekends in the fall, but now they's just hard thataway. I go over to Harry's sometimes, which helps a little bit.

I walked Elliedine to school every day and I walked her home. We didn't want no chance of anything more happenin' to her. She's my sister and I'll kill anybody what wants to hurt her. I don't care how old or how big he is. Ain't nuthin' could stop me short of me gettin' killed myself.

Elliedine is healin' up in a way. She might never

be the same, but she's startin' to get on with life. Uncle Sedg knowed a man what had had his arm shot off in the war and wasn't never the same as before, but he got on with life. Sometimes I can get Ellie to talk about her schoolwork. Then I tell her about mine. I ask her for help with things I don't really need help with, to make her think of things outside herself. Sometimes it don't seem like it helps. But I got nuthin' more important.

I got to thinkin' about how both the sun and Elliedine was shinin' bright last summer, but now don't neither one shine much. The sun just pokes its face in for a little while these days and even then it's as weak as a forty-year-old horse. I looked up and spoke to him as if he was a person.

"Mister Sun, you make plants strong and happy and plants make animals and people strong and happy. Come back warm and bright, and shine on Elliedine and make her strong and happy agin."

But Mister Sun didn't pay no mind. He stayed weak and done went hidin' by five o'clock.

THAT NIGHT, Pa and Uncle Sedgwick was talkin' more about the war in Europe.

"It was bad enough what Mr. Hitler is doin'. But now the Reds done escalated it, Mason," Uncle Sedg said. "They done attack little Finland. They is so big, but they ain't never satisfied and wants more and more."

"You hear what the U.S. done about it? Roosevelt sent in a squad of volunteer soldiers—eight of 'em. I don't understand that Roosevelt. Eight ain't enough for a army to notice. More like they's enough to clean a latrine."

"It ain't nuthin' more than a symbol, Mason. It just shows what side the U.S. is on. It's about time somebody did somethin' to show the Soviets they can't get away with their poachin' forever."

"Well, Mrs. Roosevelt, she's awful friendly with the Reds," Pa said. "I don't think the U.S. is really gonna do nuthin'. What worries me is eight men ain't enough to do Finland no good but it could make the Reds awful mad. I don't want to make other countries mad at us. Like Charles Lindbergh said, we should just hunker down and let 'em fight it out."

"That ain't what Lindbergh said, Mason," Uncle Sedgwick said.

"Pa," I said. "Who're the Reds and what're they poachin'?"

"Why, Ronson, the Reds is com-oo-nists. That means the guv'mint owns everthing, includin' the farms. The guv'mint takes all the crops and mebbe gives some of what farmers raise—their own food—back to them if'n they feels like it. One time, six or seven years ago, there was a bad year and not enough food growed for everbody. All the powerful people in the guv'mint was Russians. They just let men from the little countries that they had took over sit with them in whatever they call their congress, but don't let them really do nuthin'. Anyway, that year the guv'mint took all the crops from one of the little countries, called Yu-krain, and sent it back to Russia, and the folks in Yu-krain done starve to death. It was worse than when the damnyankees burned all the crops in Georgia so the folks would starve. In the Yu-krain, millions of folks died. It was as big as if every single God-lovin' person in Virginia starved to death, if y'all can imagine that."

"Gosh, Pa," I said. "That's awful. But what's this poachin'?"

"Ronson, they takes land from other folks like Sedgwick takes a chicken from the college coops when we gets hungry enough."

Uncle Sedg, he'd been holdin' in words what was bubblin' up inside 'til he was about to pop. Pa's words finally squoze him to pop.

"God damn it, Mason, is you accusin' me of stealin'?"

"Oh, simmer down, Sedgwick. I get as hungry as you do. I wasn't accusin' you of nuthin'."

"But, Pa," I said. "Is Uncle Sedg like the Reds?"

Uncle Sedgwick was gettin' all steamy, but Pa answered fast.

"No, it's different, Ronson. When we don't have enough to eat, Sedgwick may take one chicken out of thousands. They don't even notice the difference. The Reds, they ain't hungry for land cuz they already got more than they can use. It's more like if the college what already had thousands of chickens stole one more from a fambly what had only ten."

"Ma would say yer still stealin', and stealin' is wrong," I said.

Uncle Sedgwick couldn't stay shut up no longer.

"It's the difference between sharin' and stealin', Ronson. When people is in need, everbody ought to share. When I take a chicken, I just help 'em share cuz they ain't got the mo-rality to do it theyselves."

"That's what the com-oo-nists say, Sedgwick," Pa said. "Gotta give everbody the same to live on. Don't matter if they worked hard or just sat on their asses."

Uncle Sedg was gettin' hotter and hotter.

"That's what they SAY, Mason, and I got no quarrel with the idea of givin' everbody enough to eat. But it ain't what they DO. Them folks in power, they take everthing and split it up 'twixt theyselves and let the folks what don't got the power go to hell. I say the Reds isn't real com-oo-nists."

"Is you a com-oo-nist, Uncle Sedg?" I asked.

"Shit, no, Ronson," Uncle Sedgwick answered. "But I can understand their ideas. That's what this country's about, Ronson. We can look at all the different ways to make a guv'mint and vote to change ours to better if we wants to. Other countries, they's stuck in one way and can't change."

"It looks to me like we need a change," Pa said, "but it ain't changin'."

Uncle Sedgwick calmed down and stopped sputterin'.

"I gotta agree with you, there, Mason. You done hit the nail square on the head."

On Sunday mornin', I was over at Harry's. Doctor Hillson had already read the funnies with him and was sittin' readin' from a magazine-lookin' booklet he called a chemical journal. He showed me one of them once. It looked to me like Chinese, what with all those big and little letters hooked together with lines this way and that. I couldn't see how he could read it. Well, he did spend a hour or two on one page sometimes.

So I started readin' the funnies myself.

"Lookee here, Harry," I said. "It's sayin' Flash Gordon wasn't in a different century like Buck Rogers after all. He was just in a different place in space. He's decided to come to Earth to fight the evil Red Sword. Do you know what the Red Sword is?"

"Sure, Ronson. It's symbolic for the Soviet Union."

I could almost hear a thump in my head from everthing fallin' together.

"They's the ones called the Reds. They's com-oo-nist," I said, feelin' all excited I'd put it together. "They've invaded Finland."

"That's right, Ronson. Flash Gordon is coming in to help Finland."

"He's not the only one helpin'," I said. "President Roosevelt done sent a troop of eight soldiers over to show we's backin' them up."

"No," Harry said. "Where'd you get that idea?"

Doctor Hillson looked up from his journal.

"He's right, Harry. Roosevelt has done that. It's a symbolic move to show international disapproval of the Soviet invasion."

Harry looked at me like I'd throwed water on him, his mouth hangin' open. I felt all warm and glowy all over cuz for once't I knowed somethin' he didn't. I got to listen more to Pa and Uncle Sedg when they talk. It was fun to learn somethin' new.

"Doctor Hillson, does that mean we could go to war with the Reds?" I asked.

"I doubt it, Ronson. It isn't threatening enough to provoke a war. It's more political than military."

"It's sort of like when a bull is busy eatin', you

poke it with a twig. It knows you poked it, but it would rather eat. But if you poke it hard with a big stick, it'll turn on you."

Doctor Hillson's face lit up with a big smile. Then he tipped his head and looked at me real hard, like he was thinkin' all deep. I looked back for a spell, but then looked down. Finally, he spoke to me.

"That's a very apt analogy, Ronson. It's clear you see how different political forces cause different outcomes in relations between nations. Very good."

Well, did you ever? A high-up man what knows everthing sayin' I done good! I felt all glowy inside then. But Harry, he got a little red in the face. I don't know if he was a little jealous or just surprised I knowed stuff he didn't. But he didn't say nuthin'. Harry was more of a pok-ee than a pok-er.

ONE DAY I'd just come acrost the field to Harry's and was tryin' to shake mud clods off my feet without losin' my shoes—it'd rained durin' the night—when Harry called to me. It was loud enough that anybody could hear it, but in a whisper sort of sound so anybody what heard it would know they wasn't s'posed to hear it. It's kind of dumb, cuz if you got a secret, you're tellin' everbody.

"Ronson," he said, "look at this."

I looked around and didn't see him. But then I saw his face pokin' across the door jamb of what the Hillsons called the playhouse.

There's this little old house, all gray with age and wood goin' warped, behind the Hillsons' house, just across from the sandbox where Harry got his soldiers and trucks. It's one big room when you go in with a stair at the back what goes up to another one big room on top. I guess they had a kitchen, eatin' room, and sittin' room all together downstairs with beds up above. I asked Miz Hillson one time if it'd been slave quarters, but she said it wasn't old enough to have been built in slave days. She said it must have been servants' quarters mebbe fifty years ago. The Hillsons done give it to Harry to play in and keep toys and models and stuff. The neighborhood kids use it, too, cuz they ain't got one of their own.

Anyway, the little kids in the neighborhood play in there sometimes and the big kids have meetin's. Harry, he got a electric train in there and a airport for the balsa wood models he makes. Upstairs, we can get all alone with no grownups to see us or hear us. We used to have clubs with secret passwords and stuff like that. Harry was great on secret passwords, but I couldn't see the point. All the kids knew the password and didn't nobody else want to come to the club meetin' anyway.

One time, about three years ago, we had a big meetin' with all the club to decide what the password would be and how we could keep somebody out if he didn't know it. Mac Holdaway, he wanted the password to be "open sesame" from a book what sounded to me like knights over in the A-rab lands. Mac had a stub of pencil and slip of paper in his pocket and wrote it down. I looked at it.

"That sez 'open see-same,'" I said, my mouth workin' away at sixty before my brain got in gear. They all laughed at me. I felt dumb and mad and went in the corner and sat down on the floor. They didn't pay me no more mind, which made me all the madder, and started talkin' about how was they goin' to keep out a kid what didn't know the password.

"We have to make a trap door with a latch and padlock on it," said one.

"Then nobody that does know the password could come in either," said another.

"And, anyway," said Harry, "by the time somebody's there and we ask if he knows the password, he's already inside."

That put a cork in it. They all stood there, dumb like a scatter of cats got all their tongues. So I done come back from the corner and told them.

"If somebody comes and don't know the password, we just won't speak no secret club stuff. In fact, we don't speak at all. We'll just all stay where we is, quiet like, not lookin' at him, 'til he gets embarrassed and goes away."

"Yes. Send him to Coventry!" Mac said. I didn't know how we could send him anywhere, but all the others just nodded like they agreed, so I didn't say nuthin' more.

But we've all got past that stuff. Nowadays, Mac and the bunch talk about who's on which football team for the afternoon game in the Holdaways' big front yard. My thoughts keep goin' off on other things than where they started. I was just thinkin' about the one time I was smarter than all those town kids.

Harry stuck his head around the door jamb and made that dumb whisper-yell. I went into the playhouse.

"What's goin' on, Harry?"

Harry walked to the stairway at the back of the room and went up. I follered. When we got to the top, he turned, his face all lit up.

"Ronson, when I biked downtown to get some glue for my models, I saw something at the newspaper stand. It was pretty much covered up by other magazines, but I pulled it out. It was all about how bad life is in Russia, that is, in the Soviet Union. It had a picture of a party among poor people in Moscow. You won't believe it. It cost a whole dime, but I bought it. I had forty-three cents saved up. Let me get it."

He went to the wall and loosed a board and pulled a small magazine out from behind it.

"My folks wouldn't want me to be reading this, so I hid it up here."

"Why wouldn't your folks want you to read it?"

"They think I'm as innocent as a child. My mom tries to shield me from all sorts of information that I already know. I spend a lot of time in the library. The librarian, Lucy Lee Lancaster, is a friend of Mom's. Mom has her steer me to books for children and youths. She leaves me to read them. Then I go back in the stacks and read all sorts of books."

"Like what?" I asked.

"Well, for example, this magazine describes the poverty and insufferable living conditions in Moscow. I have already read about such conditions in Chicago, here in the United States. Upton Sinclair wrote a book about the stockyard business and the people working in them. It was just as bad as Moscow. And books by Charles Dickens tells about poverty in London and scoundrels that hoodwink and cheat poor children."

"Well, if they's in books for everone to read, why don't folks do anything about it?" I asked.

Harry frowned and wiggled his head from side to side.

"Shucks, Ronson, I don't know. In Dickens's books, the poor boy, the main character in the story, always gets rescued by somebody rich. Then the reader follows him in his new life and never again thinks of all the other boys he left behind."

When I thought about that, I felt a taste in my mouth as bitter as raw dandelion greens.

"The rich do little-bitty things to look like they's helpin' the poor," I said. "But they don't give a rat's ass for real."

"Yes, I read in one place where the rich man, hearing that a poor person had starved to death, said, 'One less useless mouth to feed. It's a decrease in the surplus population.' It's almost enough to convert me to socialism."

We sat, quiet, thinkin' how the gov'mint wasn't workin' the way it should. I picked up the magazine and thumbed through it. It opened to a picture of the party, or whatever it was, that Harry had spoke about.

"This looks like what I seen one time off toward the Kentucky line when we was visitin' some of Ma's kin," I told Harry. "My folks took me and Elliedine away fast as greased lightnin', but I seen what was goin' on in one blink. They was a moonshine still behind the house and the folks there had been into the white lightnin' right smart. They was fallin' down and takin' their clothes off and playin' around with each other somethin' fierce."

"That's just what this picture shows," Harry said. "There are people passed out, bottles all over the place, and—look at that—girls with hardly any clothes on."

Harry's eyes was big and he seemed all excited.

"Do you think about girls, Ronson?" he asked, soundin' all hopeful.

I had to think about what I thought, if that don't sound too crazy.

"Yeah, sometimes."

"I never used to, but when I saw this, I couldn't take my eyes off it. I started to get hard—you know—down there. Do you ever get hard?"

"Yeah, sometimes. Nowadays," I said.

Harry was shruggin' his shoulders and kind of wigglin' around. He couldn't stand still. I could see he had a bulge in his pants.

"I've heard," I said, "that there's girls what will do it for money."

Harry looked like he'd been hit in the face with a wet catfish.

"No-o-o," he said, drawin' it out.

"Sure as shootin'," I said. Thinkin' about it, I was gettin' a little hard, too.

It was too much for Harry. He unbuttoned his pants and took it out.

"Can I see yours?" he asked.

By then I was as ready as he was and I unbuttoned and took mine out, all parts of it. Well, we looked at each other's and rubbed our own a little and then a little more. I have to tell you that I was thinkin' how I'd like to rub his a little, but I didn't know how he'd take that, so I didn't say nuthin'.

After a while, with nuthin' happenin', we got tired of it and quit and put them back in our pants.

"I wonder how old you have to be to take a girl," Harry said.

"I don't know, but I think we're gettin' close," I said. "But, you know, Harry, sometimes when I get all spunked up, I think about what happened to Ellie. It don't seem right to want it when it hurt her so bad."

Harry hung his head the way he does, feelin' guilty, I guess.

"What are we going to do about that, Ronson? The grownups aren't doing anything at all. Maybe we should find a way."

"Mebbe they done somethin' and didn't tell us, Harry. Let's go ask Uncle Sedgwick. He'll be about gettin' home by now."

Harry put the magazine back in its hidey-hole and we started toward his house. We took the long way around by road, cuz so much mud in the field would stick to your shoes that you got tuckered in twenty paces—if the mud didn't first pull your shoe right off your foot.

～

UNCLE SEDGWICK HAD JUST COME in and was sittin' down for his after-work cigarette. He said that it helped him get through the day thinkin' about how he could have a smoke when he finished. He didn't pay us no mind. He stretched his bones all out this way and that and then sat down in the rocker chair on the porch. He took his cigarette pack out of his pocket real slow like. He wiggled his finger in the pack, pushin' a cigarette to the front. Then he pulled the cigarette out of the pack and stuck it between his lips real slow like. He pulled a match from his pocket, struck it on his overall leg, and lit up real slow like. He took a long suck and let the smoke out real slow like. It was all like he was tryin' to make it last. He sighed big and deep, and then looked at us like he was seein' us waitin' there for the first time.

"Afternoon, boys," he said. "What's on yer minds?"

"Uncle Sedgwick, I'm still mad about what they done to Elliedine," I said.

"So are we all," he said. He waited.

"We want to do somethin' about it," I said. "We want to GET those peckerwoods."

"So do we all," he said.

"Is that all ye got to say, Uncle Sedgwick? Ain't you riled?"

"Hell, yes, boy. We's all of us riled. We talk about it every day."

"Talk," I said, soundin' kind of bitter. "Not do?"

"Do what, Ronson?" he said, gettin' his dander up a notch. "We ain't figgered what to do. We done made a whole bunch of different plans, but somethin' stops every one. We don't know how much power those caydets got, who they know. We barely got enough to eat as it is. We can't go losin' a job durin' this here de-pression. See, once we take any action, the cat's out of the bag and we can't put it back in. If they's got daddies what knows somebody high up, they could get away with it and get yer pa and me fired. We can't undo what we done if we find we done the wrong thing."

"But, Uncle Sedgwick, we gotta do somethin'."

"Yer ma's done been cryin' her eyes out. Yer pa done grind his teeth 'til they're breakin'. And I go and chop wood every night cuz I gotta break somethin'. Look at it this way, Ronson. Think of the fambly all put together as a person. This person done got a bone broke. Now what's more important —healin' the bone to go on livin' or findin' the person what done broke the bone. We're tryin' to get through it, to get Ellie to heal. Sure, we want to get them fellers. We just ain't figgered how we can be sure to win without losin'."

He stopped, looked down at his shoes for a spell, then looked up at me. I never seen him look so tired. His eyes was sunk and his face had folds and lines like a old man.

"Do you have somethin' in mind?" he asked.

We didn't know what to say. We didn't have no plan neither. The grownups don't know what to do. And we think we kids can do it? I tried to hunker down but didn't have nuthin' to hunker under.

"We don't know. But we want to do somethin'," I said.

"Ronson, Harry, y'all got good hearts to want to, but even if you knew what to do, you don't even know who they is!"

Well, that put the lid on the jar. We was not only kids tryin' to play a grownup game but we hadn't even thought it out. We ain't done nuthin' to find out who they is. I felt so stupid. Harry was hangin' his head.

"Thanks, Uncle Sedg," I managed to mumble.

We walked out into the winter, but I felt colder inside than outside.

THE NEXT WEEK was the last week of school before Christmas. Folks was puttin' up Christmas trees and hangin' pretty gewgaws on them. Folks what had money was all buyin' Christmas gifts. My family was tryin' to figger what they could make out of odds and ends for presents. Except Elliedine. She couldn't climb out of her sad-valley.

"Ronson," Harry said, "We have to find out who

they are. What sort of thing we can do depends on who they are, where their vulnerabilities lie, and what defense resources they have."

Lord a mercy! What a mouthful. If Harry keeps on growin' that kind of talk, when he's grown up nobody will have any idea what he's sayin'. But I got the idea—we gotta find out who they is before we can plan.

I realized I was lookin' at him with my trap hangin' open. I shut it.

"Can you get Elliedine to describe them to you?" he asked.

"She don't talk much, Harry. But I been gettin' her to talk about school stuff. Mebbe this long after I can get her to tell what she knows.

THE NEXT DAY when I was walkin' Elliedine home from school, I asked her if she wanted to get the fellers what done her. She stopped cold in the middle of a step and looked at me. I ain't never seen her look like that. It wasn't my sunshine sister lookin' at me. It was a hungry hunter, mean and determined.

"Of course I do, Ronson. More than anything in my life."

"Then, Ellie, you gotta tell me how I can find

out who they is. We gotta know that before we can make a plan to get them."

She didn't move. She stood there like she was a statue made out of stone. I thought, oh, Lord, my sweet sister done turned to stone. But she started talkin', stronger and faster than she had since she got hurt.

"I'll never forget them—everthing about it. One was light, almost white-headed with blue eyes, and the other had a big black spot on the left side of his face just in front of his ear. He had one of those wrinkles in his chin."

"Did they say their names?" I asked.

"The white-headed one called the other one Luther and moley-face called the whitey feller Waylon. And they didn't talk mountain. They talked like they's from Tidewater. That's all I know. They didn't say their last names any."

She turned, said "That's all I know" agin, and started walkin'. Fast.

I stood there for a minute, bells all a-clangin' in my head. Godamighty! I knowed them fellers! They's the ones what was workin' over that poor rat on the drill field last fall. The mean ones.

I turned and ran to catch up with Ellie. I couldn't wait to tell Harry who they was.

7

JANUARY 1940

It had just turned into nineteen and forty. The snow was deep. Pa and Uncle Sedgwick went off to work in the barns. They had brung all the farm animals inside so they wouldn't freeze or thirst to death. When I took lunch over to Pa and Uncle Sedg on Saturday, it was so cold in the barn I felt warmer out in the snow. It was confusin' and messy with all the animals cooped up. The critters didn't like it any more'n we did and they let everbody know about it, which Pa and Sedg couldn't do so's not to lose their jobs. The animals was mooin' and brayin' and snickerin' and stampin' and fartin' and shittin' and makin' all kinds of noise. They was pushin' and buttin' and gen'rally actin' like animals. Which of course they was. And the men was cursin' and herdin' and separatin' and feedin' and gen'rally actin' not all that much different. I got out of there as soon as I could and felt sorry for Pa and Uncle Sedgwick.

But then, evenin' come and we was all cooped up in our little shanty and it was almost as bad as the barn, except it warnt quite so cold. Everbody was gettin' in each other's way, and the "s'cuse me's" was comin' faster'n the "praise the Lords" at a revival meetin'. We did have time to do things, which we didn't in plantin' or harvestin' times. Uncle Sedg was a whiz at the guitar—which he called his git-fiddle—and he taught me and Elliedine somethin' about how to play.

A lot of the farm help what lived up and down our row of houses went for the moonshine when they couldn't get out, and we heard a whole load of men shoutin' and women cryin' and like that. But Pa and Uncle Sedgwick loved their family more'n they loved a jug, and they sat with us and tried to do somethin' with the time. Ma put on like it didn't make no difference to her, but I saw her face when we heard the goin's on, and I knowed she loved Pa and Uncle Sedg for not bein' like that.

There was times when the wind blew so hard I could swear it came right through the wall. You could feel it if you put your hand up close to the wall. The wind always blows in Blacksburg. It's fine other parts of the year, even nice. But in winter, it's fierce. The weather starts way up in Canada and blows down hundreds of miles. I don't believe it's true what some folks say, that West Virginians send it down cuz they's traitors. We disrespect them cuz they split off from Virginia in 1861 to go with the damnyankees. That makes them worse than other damnyankees and folks like to blame things on them. But fact is, they really ain't that different from us.

But when the wind ain't blowin' from the north, it's blowin' from the east or the west. One or t'other. Pa sez that Blacksburg sits on what some call "the little continental divide." He sez that rain on the west side of the Blacksburg golf course would wash a broke tree branch downhill into New River. It would float north to the Gauley River, then to the Kanawa River, then to the Ohio River. Then it would change the way it goes, floatin' southwest to the Mississippi River and then to the Gulf of Mexico. But rain on the east side of the golf course would wash that branch downhill into the Roanoke River. It would float southeast through Virginia, through North Carolina, to Albemarle Sound, on the coast of North Carolina, and then into the Atlantic Ocean. I guess I didn't sleep in geography class, now, did I?

Sometimes in the winter, we get a thaw. It gets to where a body can go outside and come back in without frozen balls. Uh-oh. Ma wouldn't want me to say that. Anyway, on days like that we can sit on the porch. Uncle Sedgwick plays his git-fiddle and we all sing songs. Harry's told me he can hear us singin' from across the field. He sez he loves it. He ought to come over and sing with us, but for some reason the idea don't sit well with him. The Hillsons don't never sing, except carols at Christmas. I feel a little sorry for 'em that way.

We sing pretty much the same songs each time, like we don't know more'n a dozen. We sing "Comin' 'Round the Mountain," which I never understood. Why is who comin' 'round? But it's got a good tune. And we sing "You Are My Sunshine," about a slave beggin' his master not to sell his woman away from him. And like that.

I always feel sad when we sing "Sunshine." It ain't right to break families into pieces, apart from what the damnyankees did. A lot of men—Uncle Sedg sez half a million—died in that fight between the states, and one thing they died for was so Americans couldn't take a woman from her man or a child from his folks. That can't happen no more in the U.S. of A.

Anyway, we don't see many black folks in Blacksburg. There is some, I know, cuz I've seen them at the movie house. They can't sit with white folks, of course, but there's a second balcony way up high in the Lyric The-ayter. There's a stairway goin' up with a door to it at the left side of the big marquee over the entrance. They goes and stands there and waves at the girl sellin' tickets. She pushes a buzzer what tells the ticket taker and he comes out and takes the black folks' money and lets them in to walk up the back stairs. Mebbe some folks don't think that's the way it should be, but truth is Mister Kelsey, the manager, charges them less than the white folks. They goes up and sits in the high balcony and that way can see a movie picture. I once heard the ticket taker say the horses on the screen look like mice from way up there. Anyway, I seen some black folks at that door. But there ain't many and I don't know where they live or what work they do to make money. They seem real nice. I sez hi and they sez hi and we nod.

But some folks in town treat 'em bad. There's a lawyer with a big house down on Clay Street near the Huckleberry trestle what had a boy Harry used to play with sometimes, name of John Neal. I was over there one time with them when a little black boy was walkin' up the street just goin' by. The pa was out on the porch pettin' his little bulldog when he seen this black boy. He pushed his bulldog and sez, "Sic'm. Sic'm." The bulldog run out after the black boy. He started to run but couldn't run fast enough. The bulldog caught him and bit him. The black boy was cryin' and cryin'. He turned to the pa and sez, "I'll get you. Just wait. I'll get you." And the pa just laughed and laughed. I felt awful bad about it, but there was nuthin' I could do. Just nuthin'.

I asked Pa about black folks and other folk what's different.

"It's complicated, Ronson. Black folk what's raised here are different but not real different from us, but there's other black folk what come from other places that are a sight different."

"I seen a geographic magazine over to Harry's what shows brown folk and yellow folk and Lord knows what. Them's foreigners, ain't they? Even more foreign than damnyankees?"

Pa just shook his head kinda slow.

"It gets real hard to figger, Ronson," he told me, "cuz some foreign folks is more foreign than other foreign folks. I seen a lot of different folks when I was in the war in France. There was colored soldiers from Africa and from India. All sorts of mix-up in the French Foreign Legion. And regular-lookin' soldiers from Australia. And, of course, from England, which was just a boat ride away from France. They looked different and talked different and had different uniforms, but inside they was all the same as us."

"And you was all fightin' the Germans."

"Well, Ronson, truth is, the Germans was the same, too. They was just young men from their farms caught up by the guv'mint and made to go fight. All colors of folks and ways of talkin' on both sides, didn't make no difference. They all did the soldierin' they had to do, but all they wanted was for the war to be over so they could get home to their famblies. I think wars is sometimes made to kill men so the big companies what make guns can get rich. That's awful evil."

"Then why go, Pa?"

"The guv'mint convinces everbody that the other side is bad and we gotta fight them to save ourselves. And the guv'mint on the other side sez the same thing to their folks. But they lie. They said that the war I was in would be the last and would end all wars if we'd just win it. Well, we did and lookee now—there's another war in the same place between the same people. No, Ronson, I've come to believe that we's all alike down deep."

"But ain't they the enemy, Pa?"

"Enemy? Who's the enemy, Ronson? The British was at one time, but now they're not. The damnyankees was, but now they're not—or at least not the war kind. Are the folks from Tidewater Virginia enemies? No, but to us, those two animals you found out hurt Elliedine are. That makes them enemies in amongst friends. And over in Kentucky, there's neighbors killin' each other—the Hatfields and McCoys, for example. I thought about it a lot, Ronson, and here's how I see it. We should treat everone with respect. But they has different ways, so we just gotta be careful about trustin' them all the way lessen they's one of us."

THE NEXT TIME I was with Harry, I told him what Pa had said.

"He sounds pretty wise, Ronson. I must say that he exudes more dignity than any rich man I've ever met."

Harry always comes up with these words don't nobody else know. He gets them from all those books he reads. He reads too much. Or maybe I should read more. Wouldn't it be somethin' if I could learn a word he don't know? Mebbe I'll try that.

"Well," I said, "he don't talk a lot, but when he does talk, a body better listen."

"You probably remember some of the kids in school with us that looked different," Harry said. "We had several because their dads came to teach at the college. Remember Shannon O'Conner that had the bright, very red hair? He was from Ireland. And the Italian boy, Marco Battalini."

"I remember 'em. They was just regular kids, but I remember how mean the other boys was to them. Nobody would play with Shannon. They just cut him out of everthing. He tried not to cry, but I seen his eyes all wet."

"Yes. And Marco. They called him Wop-alini and laughed at him in that sing-song rhythm. He tried to fight, but then just broke down in tears. I don't think your dad would have liked that."

"No, he wouldn't. And neither would your pa."

"No." Harry thought a minute. "I guess we have pretty good fathers, Ronson."

"We do. We's lucky, Harry."

I thought about it. "Y'know what? Some of the mean kids was also foreigners. Remember Stevie Lewiston? Whose pa done come down from Maine to teach? He was somethin' else, always treatin' us like we was stupid."

"Oh, yes. Who could forget him? Do you remember the time in Mrs. Haller's history class when he gave a northern answer to a southern question?"

I chuckled. "Miz Haller asked a question that wanted 'The War Between the States' as a answer. And he said 'The Civil War.' I remember how Miz Haller squintified her eyes real small and stuck her head forward ever so much, like a boar gettin' ready to charge."

"Hoo," hooted Harry. "And she asked, 'Wha-a-at?,' drawing the word out. He was as smart as he was mean. He saw what she wanted and that he was getting under her skin."

"So he sez, 'The Rebellion of 1861,' and she ups and sends him to the principal's office."

We both snickered at the memory and sat a minute.

"Y'know?" I said. "Some mean kids grow out of it and are good when they grow up. But other kids stays mean when they grow up."

"I wonder what makes the difference," Harry said.

Then it hit me, the idea of growin' up mean. It hit me like I run smack into a fence post. I had plum forgot about those two cadets.

"I'll tell ye somebody what growed up real mean—them cadets what hurt Elliedine."

"You're so right, Ronson! They're a couple of snakes all right."

"What're we gonna do to catch 'em, Harry?"

"Somehow we have to find out who they are."

"Oh, geez, Harry. I plum forgot to tell ye. Elliedine done tell me somethin' about 'em."

"And you didn't tell me?" Harry asked, soundin' real put out and a little mad.

"They's the two we saw last fall runnin' that poor feller back and forth across the drill field. She told me what they looked like real careful. And she heard their names. The one what had the whitey hair is called Waylon and the one with the wrinkle in his chin and a mole in front of his ear is called Luther."

"They're the ones, all right, Ronson. Whitey and Moley are the names we decided to call them last fall."

"So now we knows who they is."

"No, Ronson. We have clues—appearance and Christian names—but we have to find out their family names and where they're barracked if we're going to do anything to them."

"That's true, Harry. That's true," I said, and I felt like hangin' my head the way he does. But when I realized what I was doin', I straightened up tall and pushed out my chin like Pa.

"I figgered a way to get them," I said.

"What's that?"

"I seen in a western movie one time where they tied a rope across a trail and the other feller's horse tripped over it and throwed him off and he was knocked out when he hit the ground. We could tie a wire, thin so they don't see it in time, like that and trip 'em and hurt 'em."

Harry looked at me like I was the dumbest bunny in the pasture.

"Sure," he said. "We just ask them what path they're going to take and when, and they don't catch on to that, and we keep everybody else from going that way, and we make sure they're walking parallel so both trip at the same time, and you figure out how to trip them so they fall on their head and not just a shoulder."

Well, when he put it like that, I could see there might be some troubles in that idea. I didn't say nuthin'. I just looked off at the Blue Ridge Mountains what had snow on them this time of year.

"I have a better idea," he said. "We go to the roster where they keep demerit lists for the cadets and we add a whole bunch of demerits to them."

He smiled, lookin' all superior-like. I vowed to make him feel as dumb as I felt.

"Sure," I said, just like he had. "We knows where the de-merit list is kept and how they's writ down and what to write for the reason you give the de-merits and how to sign a upperclassman's name for them. And then we just walk in as if we owned the place and start writin' on their list, two kids what ain't wearin' uniforms."

Well, that squashed his idea, too. What we shoulda been doin' was figgerin' how to learn their last names, but we was just kids still. I tol' myself: We got a grown-up problem, so we gotta think like grownups. I thought how much I'd learned listenin' to Pa and Uncle Sedgwick talk about problems. I promised myself I'd listen more to grownups and mebbe learn how they figger out problems. We just didn't know how to start.

THAT NIGHT, Pa and Uncle Sedg were talkin' about a problem. I perked my ears up like a fox hearin' houn' dogs.

"Sedgwick, when all this snow melts and runs off and then we get spring rains, it's goin' to take the new topsoil from those slopin' fields in the southwest corner with it—wash it right away. We oughta figger a way to stop it. If the topsoil is gone from them, they won't match the flatter fields in crop-growin' exper'ments."

"I hear what yer sayin', Mason, but it ain't our worry. If the aggie teachers want us to do somethin', they'll tell us."

"If we had a good idea that helped out, mebbe they'd remember it when layoff time comes."

"Mebbe. Mebbe. I wouldn't put money on it."

"Anyway, it'd be a good thing to do, Sedgwick."

"Well-l-l," he strung the word out real long. "When we was in France, I remember seein' a photo picture from Italy. There's mostly mountains there. They made what they called terraces. They made a little wall where the hill sloped down and moved the high dirt down on top of the low dirt so there was a level strip of land. God knows there's enough rocks in our fields to make a little wall."

"That's a right smart idea, Sedgwick, except where would we get the manpower to build the walls and move the dirt? We ain't got enough as it is. And we'd have to move off the topsoil, level out the base dirt, and then put the topsoil back. More manpower. And a lot of gradin' machines we don't got."

"Well, I don't got another idea."

They sat quiet for a couple of minutes. Then Uncle Sedg started up agin.

"Speakin' of water runnin' off, I heard some students talkin' today. They was tellin' about how some freshmen got even with a chickenshit sophomore caydet what was givin' 'em unfair de-merits."

"Yeah? How's that?" Pa asked.

"They snuck into his room while he was asleep and throwed a bucket of cold water on him. 'Course they run away before he seen who it was."

"I can imagine it. Even if he dries off and puts on dry nightclothes, his sheets and mattress is still cold and wet."

"And he knows they can do it agin if he don't stop bein' chickenshit. The boys I heard talkin' about it said it wasn't the first time. There's a traydition of it at the school. It's the way they keeps the upperclassmen from goin' too far."

Well, I'll tell you! My plan of listenin' to grownups was workin' right smart. I learnt a whole bunch of stuff real fast. I learnt about topsoil and about terraces. I learnt about how you can fix most anything if you got enough money, but how most things don't get fixed just cuz the money ain't there. And I learnt that if you can't fix somethin' within the rules, you can sometimes fix it outside the rules.

∼

ELLIEDINE WAS STILL all crunched up inside. She didn't sleep good and was gettin' dark around her eyes. She didn't eat good neither, just playin' with her food. Pa didn't like her leavin' food on her plate when the rest of us wasn't gettin' enough. He started to say somethin' to her, but Ma knowed what he was up to and give him a look what must've fried his gizzard up like chitlins. He held his peace.

Ma and Pa must've talked it over when I wasn't there, cuz they decided it might help to take her to church, where everbody is good—or at least pretendin' like it. Maybe she'd catch good feelin's or somethin'. It didn't work out thataway.

We goes to the Wesleyan Methodist church. That's the church for the poor folks. The other churches in town are mostly for rich people. We don't feel good goin' to those ones. They has all this highfalutin procedure and everbody has to keep real quiet. In our church, we can speak up when the preacher sez somethin' we like. At least, the Presbyterian, the Baptist, and the regular Methodist are southern churches. The E-piscopalian is a Englander and New Englander church. And there's even one called the Catholic church. There ain't many of them people here in town, so it's real small. In fact, I ain't never seen one of them Catholics, so I don't know if they looks different from us. Pa calls them crossbellies, but I don't know what that means. Harry sez his folks told him there's even more kinds of churches. They's a church for Jews and for Musselmen, but there ain't any of them people here in town. I wouldn't know one if I sat next to him on a bus. I got no idea what they look like.

Anyway, we all took Elliedine to church on Sunday. It started out OK. Everbody sez hello to us includin' Elliedine, so she brung herself to say hello back and nod and all. But she didn't smile to nobody for nuthin'.

Before long, the preacher started his speech. He done say sin is when a man and a woman lie together—he done call it a-he'in and a-she'in. He got more and more worked up about it and got a little red in the face and started yellin' about how any woman what laid with a man before they got married was goin' to Hell. Well, that didn't sit good with Ellie. She done hung her head down like a apple branch full of fruit. She didn't walk out on his sermon like I bet Uncle Sedgwick would have done in her situation. She just looked down at the floor and tried to get as little as she could. Walkin' home, she walked off fast and went ahead of us. She didn't even want to be with her own fambly.

∽

WHEN WE GOT HOME, Elliedine had already gone to the bedroom. She was lyin' in the bed, cryin'. I went in and sat on the bed and held her hand. After a while, she stopped and turned to me. Her face was all wet and swollen.

"Ronson," she said, "I can't b'lieve in no God what lets that happen to me when I can't help it and then sez I'm going to Hell for it."

"No, Ellie," I said, "that wasn't God. That was just the mean ol' preacher talkin' and he got nuthin' but a rock betwixt his ears. Ye can't pay no attention to the likes of him."

"But he's the legal preacher, Ronson. They calls him a Man of God."

I didn't know what to say. I was thinkin' fast. I had done been what churchy-folk called a 'God-fearin' boy'. In about two seconds, I moved to one what figgered I'd go straight to God and tell Him He ain't bein' fair and He shouldn't let preachers do his talkin'. So I told that to Elliedine.

"Ellie," I said, "what they calls him and whatever he calls hisself, that's just man-made-up. It don't come from God. From now on, you and I is not goin' to church. We'll go out in the forest and we'll look at the birds and squirrels and trees what we know God made all growin' happy under God's Mister Sun and we'll be closer to God than goin' through somebody what don't know no more'n we do what God is like but wants us to think he does so we'll put money we don't got in his fancy plate."

Well, that was the longest thing I'd said in a coon's life. It just come up and spilled out like when you squeeze a boot what's been left out in the rain. Anyway, Elliedine grabbed me and hugged me and held me a long time. I thought I was almost as glad as she was, cuz it'd been a long time that she wouldn't let me touch her.

Then she let go of me and crossed her arms over her chest real tight like she was tryin' to squeeze herself from a quart down to a pint.

"I feel so alone, Ronson. I feel like I don't belong nowhere no more."

"Ellie," I said, "you ain't never alone. You got my lovin' with you even if I'm off at school or somewheres. You'll always have me, whatever. Think on that whenever the world kicks you in the gizzard."

She looked up and smiled that smile of hers that tickles everbody in their hearts, and I knowed I done somethin' right for once in my life.

THE NEXT DAY, I WAS TALKIN' with her.

"Ellie," I said, "I got a idea. Let me go tell Chief Sumner what happened. If he can't put them in jail for what they done, mebbe it will scare them enough to do some good."

"You mean Highpockets, the policeman, Ronson?"

"Yeah, him. Yeah, him. He knows me. When that new stoplight at Main and College went bad one day, he was out there in the middle with a little sign what said STOP on one side and GO on a crossywise side, and he was turnin' it back and forth so's folks wouldn't bump into each other. He could have given me a ticket for walkin' when his sign said stop. But he just took me aside an' explained how it was dangerous. And another time, he caught me borrowin' a rowboat on the duck pond gettin' duck eggs for us to eat. He didn't put me in jail or nuthin'. He just told me to behave myself and don't go usin' other folks' things. He tried to act real stiff and police-like, but I seen through that. Inside, he's real nice. I think he'd want to help."

Elliedine looked at me with one of those looks girls get when I don't never know what they're thinkin'.

"No, Ronson, never. Never. Thanks for wanting to help, but no."

"Why?" I asked.

"First, I don't want the whole public to know. And the police have to write down everthing so the mayor knows they're doin' their job. What they write is public knowledge. And, second, he's the policeman for the town and I don't think he has the right to do anything at the school anyhow, unless they ask him to. So he couldn't do anything anyway."

And that closed that box. I didn't have no more ideas.

Sometime later, when I was over at Harry's, I told him about the church and Elliedine and how the preacher hurt her all over agin.

"That was just cruel, Ronson. Poor Elliedine. She didn't deserve that."

"No, she didn't. Harry, does your family go to church?"

"We go now and then. It's sort of like a lot of people go because other people go, not because it does them any good. It shows we're good members of the community, and there are church socials where we see other people we don't come across every day. I don't really know what my parents believe in detail. They believe in a higher force in the universe, but I'm pretty sure they don't accept the church rituals as other than man-made. And they certainly don't believe the minister can talk to God any better than they can."

"But the preacher spends all his time studyin' the Good Book. Don't he know more?"

"If something is unknowable, you can study it

all you want and you still won't know. I have to tell you, Ronson, I don't feel good in front of preachers. One of my earliest memories was the minister preaching. I must have been three or four years old. They sat the children down front. Maybe the minister thought the closer they were, the more touched by the spirit they would be. He was almost shouting, which my parents never did, so I was pretty scared. I remember the words like yesterday. He pointed right at us kids and said, "You were born in sin and you are damned to Hell unless you accept Jesus Christ as your Lord." I remember thinking, why is he telling me I'm bad? I didn't do anything bad. I felt very scared and just awful."

"What would your pa have done about the preacher talkin' the way he did in front of Elliedine?"

"I don't know. I doubt if he would have done anything at the time. He'd probably have tried to mitigate it afterward."

"Miti...what?"

"Made it better."

"Well, why don't you say so, Harry?"

"I did. That's what I said."

I just shook my head. Readin', readin'. "Harry, why don't you read new books, instead of all those big-wordy books what was writ a long time ago before folks knowed as much as we do? I think they used big words cuz it hides that they don't know what they're talkin' about."

"I do read new books, Ronson. The library has ordered a book I'm waiting for now. It's called *The Grapes of Wrath* by a new young writer named John ... uh ... Stein .... I forget. But it's about this depression we're in, so it's very current."

"Yeah, well, I'll see if ye talk better after that."

BILLY OLDEN WAS a neighbor boy what lived down Clay Street just after it left the college and became a town road at the brick pillars. Billy had a dog he named Petey after the mutt with the ring around his eye we seen in the movie *Our Gang*. It was a movie about a bunch of kids what was supposed to be poor, but I could tell they was just pretendin'. A person what's really poor can tell another poor. It ain't what they wear or what they say. It's how they feel inside. And it just sticks out to someone what knows.

Anyway, we was over at Billy's one day playin' with BB guns shootin' all those fierce wild Injuns—we didn't never miss, y'know—when Billy's dog, Petey, come home from the woods, whinin' and crawlin' along on his belly like he done somethin' wrong. He was mighty upset, we could tell. And when he got close, the why hit us like when the wind blowed open the door. He had had a meetin' with a polecat. My land! Such a stink. Billy called his ma and she called his pa and everbody was standin' around makin' awful faces, but nobody wanted to get close to Petey. He wanted help in the worst way, but every time he come close to a body, they backed away quicker'n if he was a rattler.

Everbody waited for somebody else to do somethin'. Finally, Billy's ma went into the house to get some stuff while his pa hooked up the hose what'd been disconnected for the winter. She came out with a big gallon tin can of tomato juice and a bottle of soap she washed dishes with. And a scrub brush.

They soaped and juiced and scrubbed the poor dog with their faces lookin' like they was emptyin' chamber pots. Then Billy's pa turned the hose on the dog. Well, bein' this was a warm day for January, the hose wasn't froze and the water come through, but, boy, it must have been cold. The poor dog let out some howls like he was bein' killed and tried to get loose to run away, but they held him tight and washed all the soap and juice off. Most of the stink went with it, but enough stayed that nobody wanted to be around the dog.

I watched as the dog got hit with the cold water and I saw him jump and wriggle and whine. A idea hit me just as hard as the hose water hit the dog. Suppose we could douse ice water on those shit-eatin' cadets—*Oh, land! I hope Ma don't hear me say that.* Wouldn't that make them miserable.

"Harry!" I yelled. "C'mere."

He come over, his eyes all big from seein' me excited.

"What?" he sez. No big words when he wasn't thinkin'. I liked Harry better when he wasn't thinkin'.

"I got a idea. Let's go back to your house so we can talk about it."

So we went back, runnin'. We went into the playhouse and I was all out of breath.

"What?" he sez agin.

"The other day Uncle Sedg was tellin' about how cadets learn a bad one to quit his bein' mean. They sneak into his room at night and throw a bucket of water on him. Well, I was thinkin' we could do that to those cadets what hurt Ellie. If we used real cold, ice-like, water, it'd make them howl like Petey."

Harry started to smile and real slow he smiled bigger and bigger. "Suppose we did that, but mixed skunk spray into the ice water."

I just chortled. I whooped. We done found a way to get at those two jackanapes.

"Harry, that's just finer'n frog fuzz," I tol' him.

Then Harry calmed down and started lookin' serious-like.

"We have to find out their names and what

rooms in the barracks they're in. And we have to find a way to do them both at once. If we did just one, they'd start guarding against it and we probably couldn't get the other one."

"But it's somethin' to shoot for."

"For sure."

And we sat there for a spell, just baskin' in the thought of gettin' at those pecks.

8

FEBRUARY 1940

Far as I could see, Harry read too much. He got all these crazy ideas and he liked to play like he was one of the folks from the book. He called it "pretend." I had enough problems without tryin' to pretend, but Harry, he just loved to go off into different lands or different times. Or both.

"Ronson, let's pretend we're cavemen facing wild beasts and we have nothing to protect ourselves except a spear and a knife, both chipped out of stone to be only a little bit sharp."

"No, let's take a gun, Harry, if we's gonna face some wild animals."

"They didn't have guns, Ronson. They weren't invented yet. They didn't have steel or gunpowder."

"Then why go there?"

"Oh, Ronson! Don't you have any imagination?"

"Them folks was just stupid, Harry. They wasn't edicated like you and I is. I don't want to be like them."

That got Harry right riled. But he didn't know what to say cuz he knowed I was right even if he didn't like it. So he just sat and boiled like a unwatched pot on the stove.

It was gettin' dark, so we went inside. Now, Harry's pa was pretty good at makin' new-fangled stuff and he done make a radio hisself. Well, radio sounds kind of went in and out. You could hear 'em one minute and then just a buzzy-hissy sound the next minute. See, the only station a ordinary radio could get was WDBJ in Roanoke forty miles away —well, mebbe thirty-three as the crow flies—and that not awful good. But Doctor Hillson, he strung a long wire way up high in a tree and sometimes his special radio could hear other stations. He couldn't count on what he'd hear. It was just luck or winds or stuff he talked about I didn't understand—like mebbe the chemistry of the air. But sometimes he could hear a strong station from Richmond or Nashville or one time even Atlanta. Some stations is stronger than others. Usually, what you want to hear is played on the weak ones you can't get and the strong ones play stuff you don't want, like preachers screamin' about how sinful you is.

Well, this evenin' the Hillsons, they was plannin' to listen to Edgar Bergen and Charlie McCarthy. Charlie was s'posed to be a dummy, a wooden boy, and Mister Bergen threw his voice down to Charlie so it sounded like they was talkin' back and forth. It was s'posed to be larrapin' good to watch. But on the radio where you couldn't see them, it was just two voices, and anybody could do that. So I didn't see what the big deal was. But they liked it.

The trouble was, it kept goin' in and out. Mister Bergen would set up for a joke what Charlie would make, but the sound would go out and you'd hear just hissin'. Doctor Hillson would spin dials back and forth and get it back, but just in time to hear folks laughin' after the joke was over. It made Harry's family all so mad. I don't know why they kept tryin'.

Sometimes they'd just listen to music. Music was different. If you missed a few notes it didn't matter so much. If you heard the same songs over and over, you could fill in the missin' pieces in your head. So the station played the new songs over and over—"As Time Goes By" sung by Rudy Vallee and "Begin the Beguine" played by Artie Shaw. My fav'rite was "Stormy Weather" sung by that colored gal, Ethel Waters.

Miz Hillson, she liked what they called classical music, what had a bunch of different instru-ments all playin' at once. Most times, I couldn't pick out the tune. But classical wasn't on much. A hour or two on Sunday afternoons was all the time Blacksburg got to hear classical music in a week.

At my place, we didn't have no radio. They cost too much. But one time, a feller Uncle Sedgwick worked with in the barns—we called all the agriculture work "in the barns," cuz they was too many different jobs and places to say where they was on any particular occasion. Anyway, this feller, he got hurt when a cow stepped on his ankle and they took him to the New Altamont Hospital in Christiansburg for Doctor A.M. Showalter to fix it. We didn't have no hospital in Blacksburg. Well, Uncle Sedg borried his radio 'til he come back from the hospital. It was some treat. We listened to music in the evenin'. Before we got the radio, we'd make the music ourselves. Sometimes of a evenin' a neighbor would have a fiddle or a guitar and we'd sing old songs. My favorite was "Way Down Upon the Suwannee," about how a slave is missin' his home and fambly. They wasn't a whole lot of music on WDBJ to hear on our borried radio, but one time we had it on near six of a mornin' when we was eatin' breakfast and we heard Roy Acuff and his Smoky Mountain Boys doin' that new song "Wabash Cannonball." We was all grinnin' like a dead pig in sunshine. But after a week Uncle Sedgwick had to give the radio back. We missed it somethin' awful.

Durin' the daytime when his pa was workin', Harry could listen to their radio. He liked to hear "The Lone Ranger" and "Melvin Purvis" and "Tom Mix," the cowboy. I guess I didn't have enough imagination, like he said, but I couldn't see why he was all excited every day to hear them. The Lone Ranger wore a mask like a outlaw and I figgered they'd shoot him on sight, but they never did. And he had a Injun sidekick called Tonto. A feller what work up in the barns who'd been a spell in Mexico told Uncle Sedg "tonto" meant "stupid" in Mex. I didn't get why he'd let folks call him that. And Melvin Purvis, he was a G-man. That means he was like gov'mint po-lice. But he spent half his time tryin' to get kids to send in box tops in trade for a tin G-man badge instead of goin' after the bank robbers. And Tom Mix? One minute people was shootin' at him and then he'd turn around and sing a song sayin' "Take a tip from Tom, go and tell your mom, Shredded Ralston can't be beat." Who stops to sing when he's bein' shot at? So I didn't listen much with Harry. When he curled up next to the radio, I just let him be.

But today was a little different. Melvin Purvis captured two fellers what had held somebody for ransom and was stickin' them in a jail cell. A thought hit me upside the head.

"Harry, y' know what I'd like? I'd like Mr. Purvis

to come to town and stick the two cadets what hurt Elliedine in that jail cell."

"Yeah, yeah!" Harry said, grinnin' like a tomcat what caught a mole.

"But it's been almost a month since we thought of the waterin' treatment for them and we ain't got nuthin' done about it. We gotta do somethin'."

"I have an idea," Harry said. "What we need to do is to look at all the cadets and pick those two out. Then we can tell what cadet company they're in. That narrows it down to something like maybe a hundred. When we subtract the freshmen that wear white rat belts and the cadet officers that have chevrons on their sleeves, we're down to half that or less. And knowing the company gives us the part of the barracks they live in."

"Well, sure. We tell them to line up in formation and we just walk up and down lookin' at them. I declare, Harry, that idea's barkin' up the wrong tree."

"No, silly. I'm not that dumb. Listen to this. On Sunday, they form up in the drill field and are marched to church. They're all there, because they're ordered to go to a service. They can pick which one, but they can't skip or adhere to a religion that doesn't have an established church. When they march in, they go single file, so we can look at each cadet one-by-one as they go past."

"S'pose they see us watchin' them. We don't

want them to know somethin' is up with us, cuz after we do it, they'd come lookin' for us."

"No, Ronson. They aren't allowed to look around when they march in. They have to look straight ahead. That way, we can stand around in the middle of the churchgoers outside and they won't see us."

"OK so far, Harry. But if we knowed which church to watch, we'd already know where they go and we wouldn't have to do it. That don't make sense."

"We check out a different service each Sunday until we hit it. There are only five churches. There's the Baptist, Christian, Episcopal, Methodist, and Presbyterian. I suppose there are even a dozen cadets or so that get away with going to Catholic mass, but it's unlikely our two go there since they're Tidewater Virginian, so we'd leave Catholic until last. That's just over a month and we're bound to find them."

"So then we know what church they go to. That ain't much help."

"No, Ronson, it is. They march by companies, so we can tell which company is marching in when they go past."

I thought about it. I couldn't see nuthin' wrong with it.

"I guess ye got a full jug there, Harry."

"But your mom takes you to your church, doesn't she?"

I thought about that.

"I'll tell her I'm goin' to yourn with you, Harry. She don't know you good, so she thinks you're the right kind of influence on me." I grinned at my humor.

Harry chuckled and nodded. "We can start with the Methodist and Presbyterian. They're both on Roanoke Street."

"I know," I said, riled that he acted like I wouldn't know. "Just a block or two from the grade school. We kin start this Sunday."

"The next step," Harry said, "will be to find their last names, what rooms they're in, and which beds are theirs in those rooms."

"How we gonna do that?" I asked.

"I think we need a spy," he said.

He'd been reading a book named *Ashenden* about a English spy by a writer name of, I spelled, M-a-u-g-h-a-m. Lord a mercy! How do you say a name like that? Anyway, Harry was all hot on spies.

"We couldn't hire a spy, Harry. They cost a lot of money."

Harry shook his head.

"O, Ronson! I'm speaking generically, not literally. You know Jimmy Manfred in our class? He has a big brother in the Cadet Corps. Maybe he could look it up for us if we give him the first names and company."

"Wouldn't that be turncoatin'?"

"No, I don't think so. He lives in town and most of the town boys are in the Cadet Corps just because it's required, not because they want to be."

"I guess we could ask," I said. "But what can we tell him about why we're askin'? Elliedine wouldn't want us to tell about what they done to her."

Harry scratched his head and thought and thought.

"We could say we were riding bicycles and they intentionally blocked the sidewalk to force us into the street. Cars were coming and it was dangerous. We want to report them."

"I guess that'd work," I said. I couldn't think of anything better.

So we went over to Jimmy's house and found his big brother, Pete.

"Pete," Harry said, "how do you feel about the Cadet Corps? Do you like it?"

Pete made a face what would scare a witch.

"It's militarism carried to the extreme. It's silly, pompous, and unrealistic. I wish I could get out of it. Why? Do you want to be a cadet?"

"No, not at all," Harry answered. "We have a problem and want some help."

He told the bicycle story.

"We heard them call each other by first names. If we gave you their names and the cadet company they're in, could you get us their last names and barracks room numbers?"

"Hm. I don't think that'd be very hard," Pete answered. "I know you, Harry, but," he turned to me, "who're you?"

"My name is Ronson Allen," I answered. "My pa works in the barns at the college. I go to school with Harry."

He nodded.

"Ronson?" He wrinkled his nose. "Where'd you get a name like that?"

I didn't know whether to be mad or not. But I guess it is a sort of strange name. And we wanted to get him to help us, so I answered.

"My ma told me once how I got my name. She'd just finished birthin' me and they had mopped up some mess with the newspaper. She was holdin' me for the first time and looked at the wet paper there on the floor and saw an ad for a Ronson cigarette lighter, and it just struck her that that was a purty name."

Pete laughed, but not mean like. He nodded and clapped his hand on my shoulder, so I guess he just enjoyed the story and didn't make no mind that my name was a little funny.

"Sure, guys, I could get the names and rooms."

"Great!" Harry said. "We'll get back to you when we find out the company."

Walking back to campus from Pete and Jimmy's house, Harry was all pleased.

"We're on the road now, Ronson. We have to start the church surveillance phase now."

It made me feel all sick and swirly inside like I had the Tennessee quickstep in my innards. It was just made worse when Harry used big words.

"What if it goes wrong, Harry? What if they find out it's us who's lookin' for 'em? They could make trouble for our famblies, not just us, which would be bad enough itself."

Harry sighed and half-lidded his eyes.

"That would be an unmitigated disaster," he said.

I felt the squeeze in my gizzard get bigger.

"A ... what? Y'all mean it would be bad, don't ye?"

"Yes, of course."

"Well, why can't ye just say it simple like, you ... you," I spit out, all sputtery like, not thinkin' of a word I could call him.

"Imperious? Pontifical?" he said, puttin' on a sneer. "I was just being precise. I'm sure one of us should be."

Well, that was just too much!

"Screw you, Harry. Just screw you."

It ain't usual for me to have what Ma called a conniptition fit. It wasn't normal, but I have to say I was fit to be tied. I turned and walked off, quick as I could.

"Ronson, wait. I didn't mean anything," he called after me. But I kept on walkin'.

I DIDN'T SEE Harry for a week. I was still riled. It got to me like a itch in the middle of my back where I can't reach.

"Ronson, where's Harry?" Elliedine asked. "I ain't seen him for a long time."

"He thinks he's too good for me," I answered. "He thinks it's his crowin' what makes the sun come up." I know I sounded bitter.

She gave me a smile, which she didn't much since she was hurt. I knowed I was goin' to give in the second I saw that smile. Elliedine's smile was the sun comin' out from behind a cloud. Nobody could resist her when she smiled.

"Oh, Ronson, you know he ain't like that. Whatever happened must have been a misunderstanding. You're friends. With a friend, you support each other even when things go wrong. That's how you know a real friend. Go back and make up with him. You'll be glad you did."

I found Harry inside playin' marbles in the empty fireplace. It was the only flat place with sides where the marbles would roll out of a circle but not go everwhere and get lost.

"I got a steelie," I told him, "that'll beat your big cat's eye."

He had a double-size marble that had different colors goin' thisaway and that through it. It had a brown spot in the middle of a green swirl, so we called it a cat's eye. It was bigger and heavier than normal marbles, so it knocked them out of the circle in bunches. But I had a steelie marble. It was heavier than his big one, so was fierce at knockin' every one it hit way out of the circle. But his was bigger across, so it hit more.

"Well, let's see," he said.

And we had a couple of games. He won one and I won one.

"Sorry I was persnickety, Harry," I said.

He looked at me and blinked.

"I don't know that word," he said.

"Well, Ma sez I'm that when I get highfalutin," I said.

He went to the bookshelf and took down the dictionary and looked under "p."

"Difficult. Demanding. Yes. You were," he continued.

His eyes lit all up.

"Thank you," he said. "You've taught me a new word."

"So y'all know some words I don't and I know some you don't," I replied. "We's even."

And we was full-up friends agin.

THAT SUNDAY, we tried the Methodist church. We gussied all up in our Sunday best so's we wouldn't stick out from the other folks outside. Though I have to say my best wasn't much better'n Harry's worst. But when they go to church, folks pretend they's all acceptin', which they ain't durin' the week, so didn't nobody give me no mind. I swow! The way folks act, they must have only so many smiles in their poke and they save them up durin' the week so's they can spend them on Sunday.

"Harry, we gotta stand on the left side of the church door so's we kin see the left side of their faces. Ol' Moley got his mark on his left cheek."

"Right you are, Ronson. Left side it is."

And we went over and stood in the middle of the folks what was shakin' hands and smilin' up a storm like they was best friends. We heard the cadence of the marchin' feet and here come a long line of cadets, four across. When they got close, you could hear one of the cadet officers sayin' "hup, ho, hup, ho" in a steady beat of time so's they'd all put their feet down at the same time. I wondered why that mattered. Mebbe it was to show them they couldn't even walk without bein' controlled. I don't know. I guess I wonder too many things.

The cadet officer called "halt, one, two" and they all stopped at the same time.

"Methodists," he said real loud, "ri-i-ight FACE. Two steps forward." The ones going to that church turned and took a couple of steps. "Lef-f-ft FACE." They turned back to face the way they started. That made two lines of cadets side by side, the main group and the Methodists.

"Methodi-i-ists, forward HARCH!" he shouted, and the cadets goin' into that building marched up the walk toward the door. Everbody else stood aside for them.

The cadet officer shouted, "Comp'NE-E-E, forward HARCH." And the rest of the cadets marched off toward the next church with their feet makin' a bumpy-bump rhythm like a drum.

We felt all excited and nervous and started lookin' hard at the cadets goin' in. One after another and another went past. I saw a couple of yellow heads, but they wasn't as light as Whitey. And I didn't see nobody with a mole and a wrinkle in his chin.

When they was all inside, we looked at each other. We was feelin' awful let down.

"Harry," I said, "could we have missed them?"

"We can't be sure," Harry said, "but it's unlikely that both of us would miss both of them. That's four chances to get a hit and we didn't. They probably go to another church."

"Yeah," I said. "We just gotta keep tryin'."

9
MARCH 1940

I'd been thinkin' about knowin' that word "persnickety" that Harry didn't. It felt so good that I figgered I'd go to the college liberry and start readin' and learn some more words. And in some ways it's better'n listenin' to grownups. Hundreds of grownups done put what they had to say in books that's in the liberry and you can pick what's got somethin' worth knowin' instead of just listenin' to whatever somebody wants to say and hopin' somethin' new pops out.

So I went to see Miss Lucy Lee Lancaster, who was the liberrian in charge. Now, Miss Lancaster wasn't a purty woman. She was sort of plain in the face, but she had a dimple in each cheek that got real deep when she smiled. Which was most of the time. More'n that, she had somethin' about her nobody else had. She moved quick, every movement. I couldn't tell if it made me more fired up or tired. And her eyes, they was so alive. They looked everwhere real fast and was just all lit up somehow. Her voice was high, but it was strong. When she said somethin', you knowed it was worth listenin' to.

I asked her, "Miss Lancaster, my name is Ronson Allen. My pa works in the barns for the college, so I got a right to come here, don't I?"

"Yes, indeed. You have every right. Welcome to you. What can I do for you?"

"I want to read some books and learn more words so's I kin understand better what folks is thinkin'."

She smiled real sweet and sez, "You've come to the right place, Ronson, and I'd help you even if you didn't have rights here. The first thing I need to know is how well you can read, so we don't get books that are below you or books that would lose you."

"I can read right smart. I know my talk ain't like the college folks, but in the books, why, it's the writer what's talkin', not me."

"I understand you just fine. And I'm very glad about your interest. I wish more young people from the barns would come here." She seemed almost excited. I couldn't figger why.

"Yes, ma'am," I said, not knowin' what else to say.

"The next thing is to learn what interests you so we don't bore you."

"Well, my friend Harry Hillson has spoke about books by fellers name of Sinclair and Dickens."

"Oh, you're Harry's friend! I'm a close friend of Mrs. Hillson. Yes, I know what you're referring to: Upton Sinclair and Charles Dickens. Let me see what I can find."

She turned and walked off toward the rows of shelves of books, more'n I ever seen in my life put together. And she walked as fast as I could run. I don't know how she did that. She went down the rows pullin' a book here and one there so fast she must have knowed every book personally. It was just a marvel how she could know so many books.

Well, when she'd got a armful, she come back and dumped them on a table.

"Sit right here, Ronson. Read the first two or three pages of each book and see what you find the most interesting. Then you can take the best book home and read it."

I spent a couple hours goin' through all the books and picked one to take. It was *The Good Earth*, by a woman name of Pearl Buck, about poor farm folks in China.

Well, I learnt more'n I could have dreamed from that book. I learnt words like "transmute" and "abundance." I learnt that the Chinese ain't that much different from us down in the poor places. And when Miz Buck said that "hunger makes a thief of anybody," why, that was just like Uncle Sedgwick when he took a chicken from the college coops. Before I read it, China was just a green patch on a map in a schoolbook. Now it was real and the Chinese people was real.

I couldn't wait to try out some of my new words on Harry. I was waitin' until I heard somethin' where they would work natural like. One day walkin' to school, when Harry was talkin' about the two sunovabitches what had hurt Ellie and what we was goin' to do about them, I found a way to work in my words.

"Yes, Harry, we'll transmute their arrogance into a abundance of misery."

Well, I swow! That corked up Harry's mouth right smart and his eyes got as big as eatin' plates. He just stood there still as a stature. I think I could have knocked him over with a owl feather. Finally, he spoke, but the coin had flipped to the other side and he just talked stupid.

"What? ... What?" he said.

I couldn't put on any of that arrogance I was knockin', so I had to come out with it.

"I started readin' books, Harry. I'm learnin' some words."

He thought for a minute, then nodded, then thought some more and nodded harder.

"I'm glad, Ronson. Now we'll have more between us than ever."

THE NEXT SUNDAY, we went to the Presbyterian church and repeated our trick. The cadets came marchin' in and we looked and looked. But we didn't see Whitey and Moley. Harry was gettin' discouraged. I guess he never had a lot of disappointment in his life. Most folks would see that as somethin' good, but I reckon it made him weaker in facin' the whacks that hit everbody sooner or later. It was like the French in the second book I read. About how durin' their revolution, they was choppin' the heads off all the rich folks. The book said the poor, well, if they wasn't too poor, was healthier than the rich. They ate food what hadn't been all gussied up and God's goodness took out.

"Harry," I said, "don't be so glum. This is just two churches out of five or six. Maybe the next one will be the one."

But checkin' out another church next Sunday wasn't to be.

WHEN I GOT HOME, Ma was cryin'. Ma don't cry. When trouble comes, she stands up straight and looks it square in the eye like she was sayin' "I double dare ye." But Ma was cryin'. I turned to Pa, who was sittin' in a chair beside her, holdin' her hand and lookin' like a cloud what has dropped its rain but ain't gone away yet.

"What's happenin', Pa?" I said.

"It's Grandpa," he said, and I knowed it was Ma's pa, cuz Pa's pa'd been dead a long time. "He's real sick. Mebbe he's gonna ... not gonna make it."

Ma heard him and her cryin' got real loud for a minute, then quieted back down to little sobs.

"How bad?" I asked.

"We don't know," Pa said. "I need to ask Dr. Showalter. He's in Christiansburg, but I ain't got no way to get there."

I knowed what I had to do. The Hillsons had a telephone. So I got up real quiet and slipped out. I went across the field to Harry's house and knocked on the door. Miz Hillson answered. I felt about as small as a baby possum in its ma's pouch, but I couldn't let my feelin's stop me from helpin' Ma. I swallowed two or three times and then got it out.

"Miz Hillson, my grandpa is real sick down in Wytheville. We needs to ask Doctor Showalter about his sickness, but we ain't got no telephone. Could we use your telephone and call him and ask about Grandpa?"

"Why, of course, Ronson. Tell your mom and dad to come right over."

I felt kind of hot in the face. This was hard.

"They don't know I asked, Miz Hillson. I don't think they'd do it. I don't know what to do, but somebody's got to do somethin'."

Well, Miz Hillson just looked at me like she was lookin' holes through me, but I reckon she was thinkin'. Then she spoke.

"I'll come back with you, Ronson, and ask them myself."

My land! I was both relieved and scared! But I had done shot my marble. I couldn't do nuthin' but wait and see if it won or lost me my game. So I and she done went to my house.

"Mr. Allen, Mrs. Allen," she said, "I'm Mrs. Hillson, Harry's mother. We're very fond of Ronson. I managed to get him to tell me about your father's illness, even though he didn't want to talk about it. I know you must be frightfully worried. I would like to offer the use of our telephone to get any information about it you might need."

My pa got all red in the face. I looked at him lookin' at me. Instead of seein' eyes, I seen the end of shotgun barrels lookin' to blow me to kingdom come. So I looked over at Ma. She'd turned red, too, but her worry had growed almost as big as her pride.

"Thank you, Miz Hillson," she choked out, "but we couldn't intrude like that."

I reckoned my plan was as lost as a baby bird

what had fell from its nest. But Miz Hillson, she had a trick up her sleeve.

"No, you see, we pay a fixed fee every month for the phone, so the more calls are made, the less it costs per call. So I'd like you to use it to reduce the per-call cost to us."

Now, even I could see the holes in that argument, but it surprised me. It wasn't if it had holes. It was if it was good enough that my folks could take it without losin' their pride. And it worked. My ma and I went back to the Hillsons'.

Miz Hillson dialed the phone. Blacksburg had been chose by the phone company as a exper'-mental place to try telephone dialing, while at most other towns you had to go through a operator-girl.

Miz Hillson got the New Altamont Hospital and, after waitin' a smidgin, got Doctor Showalter. Then she handed the receiver to Ma.

Ma put it to her ear and picked up the speaker part and spoke into it. I could hear Doctor Showalter's deep voice what sounded like he was talkin' through a bucket of gravel.

I could picture him, with his big bunch of white hair and strong face. He always sounded like he was talkin' about mild weather, just as calm as could be, even when things was life and death. It went a long way to keepin' his patients and their famblies settled down. It was real easy to believe in anything he said.

Well, Ma tol' him about Grandpa down in Wytheville and he said he knowed Doctor Moore at the Chitwood Memorial Clinic down there.

"Mrs. Allen, I'll call down and ask him how things are. You just sit tight and I'll call you back in a few minutes. You're at number 307, right?"

Everbody could hear what was bein' said. Ma looked at Miz Hillson with her eyes raised. Miz Hillson nodded. "Yes, Doctor," Ma said, and she hung up.

Miz Hillson spoke up. "Mrs. Allen, I have a pot of tea almost ready. Let me fix you a cup while you wait."

Ma was right surprised. Miz Hillson was treatin' her like Sunday company. We didn't drink tea, but I reckoned she wouldn't think it polite to refuse. She said thank y'all very much. Miz Hillson went into the kitchen and came back with a tray with a pot what had steam comin' out and cups and saucers and spoons and cream and sugar. She set Ma a saucer with a cup on top and a spoon at the side and done poured her some tea. It looked like halfway 'twixt coffee and water. Then she turned to me.

"How about you, Ronson? Would you like a cup?"

I didn't never expect that! I felt all strange. I

wiggled my butt a little and looked down at the rug. I'd have give my steelie marble to know what tea tasted like. I didn't know what to say. But Miz Hillson always seemed to know.

"Of course you would," she said and put out the same setup for me.

"Help yourself to cream and sugar if you want it," she said. "I don't know how you like it."

Then she got out some kind of shiny frame, all silver, with a candle in the middle at the bottom. She took out a lucifer and lit the candle and set the teapot on the frame over top of the candle. I could see it was to keep the tea hot. I never seen nuthin' like that. Ma was watchin' with great big eyes.

Miz Hillson poured herself a cup. She put in a little sugar and cream and stirred it with the spoon. She lifted the cup up with the handle and took a sip. She did it like it was the normalist thing in the world, but I reckon she did it to show Ma and me how we was s'posed to do it.

We done the same thing she had, tryin' to look like we done it every day, but probably failin'.

I didn't know what to make of the tea. It wasn't strong like coffee. It was weak, but had a good taste, what you could taste of it. I didn't see why they bothered with somethin' so weak, but I have to say I felt better after I had drunk it. I think Ma did too.

I guessed that Ma didn't feel like sayin' much, part cuz she didn't know what Miz Hillson might want to hear about and part cuz she was feared she'd say somethin' wrong.

Miz Hillson, she just rattled on about the town and where they was gonna fix a hole in the road and when they was gonna repaint the old school and stuff like that. It was things we was all interested in some, but she picked stuff what didn't stir up any feelin's.

Ma settled down a smidgin and started to answer back, sayin' which thing the town ought to fix first.

Then the phone rang. Miz Hillson answered and then handed the receiver to Ma. It was Doctor Showalter.

"Mrs. Allen," we heard him say, "I talked with Dr. Moore in Wytheville. I'm sorry to have to tell you that your father is seriously ill with pneumonia. At his age, it's a big risk. It sounds to me like you should go down and visit him. I'm very sorry to have to say this, but it might be the last time you'll see him."

"Thank you very much, Doctor. I'll do that," she managed to say, though she was mighty choked up.

I figgered Ma was readin' between the lines as they say. She would know Doctor Showalter wouldn't say outright that Grandpa was dyin', but he made that purty clear without sayin' it. And he made it clear that Ma had to go to Wytheville.

She looked up, her eyes full of tears.

"I thank y'all very much, Miz Hillson," she said. "You've been very kind."

Miz Hillson held her arms half out, kind of invitin' Ma to get a hug, but not so much as to make her feel bad if she didn't. But Ma was too proud to let down in front of folks outside the fambly, so she turned and walked out the door.

Ma and Pa talked. Pa and Uncle Sedgwick had to work and, anyway, it was Ma's pa. Pa didn't want Ma, a nice-lookin' woman, goin' so far alone with no way to call for help if she needed it. They decided I should go with Ma. They'd have Elliedine take a note to the principal's office explainin' the situation. They was sure the school would excuse me from classes. They'd ask one of the neighbor girls if she'd walk with Elliedine to school. Pa had put a few dollars away for a rainy day and it looked like it was pourin' now. He give it all to Ma. Everbody knew she'd use as little as she could and bring back what was left.

We knowed the time the bus went through town, cuz folks often had to take it to Christiansburg to shop at Leggett's Department Store or buy graham flour in bulk or go to the hospital. You couldn't do those things in Blacksburg. When it was the right time, Ma and I done walk over to Main Street where the bus stopped just above the William Preston Hotel. It come down from West

Virginia on Route 460. It took us only about fifteen minutes to get to Christiansburg, and we hunkered down to wait for the bus what went down Route 11 through Wytheville.

There weren't two seats together when we got on, so I took a seat and Ma took one behind me. I sat next to a man in a suit. It was clear he wasn't local and he was readin' a newspaper and didn't want to talk. Ma sat next to a woman who started talkin' right off like local folks do.

She and Ma introduced themselves and told where they lived. Then the woman said she knowed Miz So-an-so and asked did Ma know her. Ma said no, but she knowed Miz Whachamacallit and asked did the woman know her. Well, they kept on askin', startin' with the closest folks they knew and movin' out to ones they knew less and less until finally they come on somebody they both knowed. Then they was satisfied.

The whole thing is, you can't trust nobody 'til you know where to put them on your shelf of friends. Once you find out that she's close to Miz Whozits, who's a cousin of Miz Whatsit who lives next door, then you know where she fits in around here and you can treat her like a neighbor. Now that they know how each other belongs, if one of them don't behave like good folks do, you go to the friend they have in common and tell what they done. Then the word gets around where they live and everbody gets to know what she done bad and her reputation burns up like a firework on New Year's. When you done got pegged, you know you gotta behave and do right.

Once they placed each other, they was great buddies and was soon tradin' recipes and sayin' how awful the young folks is these days. That kept Ma busy the whole way to Wytheville. But I was awful bored.

Truth is, I stayed bored most of the time I was in Wytheville, just waitin' while Ma visited Grandpa and talked with Doctor Moore and made arrangements for Grandpa's things after he passed.

Later on, they let me see Grandpa. Ma went to rest in a rocker on the hospital's front porch while I visited him. I held his hand and he said how big I'd grown to and told me to take good care of Ma and be a good boy. Then we didn't say nuthin' for a few minutes. We was just bein' together.

"Grandpa," I said, "was you alive when they had the War Between the States?"

"Yes, Ronson, I was alive, but I was just a boy, younger'n you is. I remember it awful strong and I remember how it was after it was over when I growed up."

He closed his eyes and was quiet. *Oh, land,* I thought, suddenly real scared, *did he die?* But he was just restin'. After a minute, he opened his eyes agin.

"Why was the war, Grandpa? Why'd they fight? I heard tell it was just to free the slaves."

"It was that, Ronson, but it was more'n that. Kind of complicated. Ye have to step back and look at what was pushin' things to happen rather than gettin' all emotional about what's right or wrong like slavery. For example, we didn't have no slaves here in the mountains. We was just runnin' our farms ourselves. I hadn't even hardly seen no colored folks. And the North, they had slaves, too, although they didn't call them that. They called them 'indentured servants.' Difference was, they was held in slavery for just a fixed number of years, not for life, and their children was born free."

"A war over that?" I asked.

"Way more complicated, Ronson. The North had more industry and dominated us money-wise. They had more people, so more men to vote in Congress's House, so they dominated us politics-wise. The only place what kept us goin' was the Senate, where there was the same number of southern and northern senators. But Kansas come along and went with the North. Then the North had the Senate, too. They could make any laws they wanted and we didn't have no more power in the guv'mint. Although it didn't look like it in what folks wrote down, for fact it was taxation without representation, which is why we had fought ourselves free from the English king eighty-some years before that. That's what us folks what didn't have slaves was fightin' about."

"So different folks had different reasons for fightin'?"

"That's right, Ronson. And a lot of northeners didn't want the war either. There was riots agin it in New Yawk City. And here in the western part of Virginia, a lot of folks supported the North. The northwestern part of Virginia split off and formed their own state they called West Virginia. A lot of Virginians still see them as damnyankee traitors."

Grandpa closed his eyes agin and made a big sigh. I wondered if I was tirin' him out too much. But I felt all excited to hear what he was sayin'. He opened his eyes and started up agin.

"The war was all a big mistake. Half a million men died in it. And after it, northerners come down and took all the power. Wouldn't let any man what served in the southern army vote. It was worse politics-wise than before the war. And they had took away our sources of makin' money, so it was worse money-wise, too. And then we had our country split into two camps, hatin' each other and refusin' to work together. Can you imagine? I'm glad that ain't never gonna happen agin."

"Well, if they shouldn't have gone to war, Grandpa, what should they have done?"

"Why, Ronson, as I sees it, they should have stayed in the U.S. and the North should have found a way to make jobs for folks without usin' slaves. Then we'd have stayed on our feet—it would have took a while—and we wouldn't have needed slaves, and then we could have done away with slavery peaceful-like. We'd have used the colored folk as workers and paid them a wage. It wouldn't have been easy, but it would have been better'n what happened by a long, long shot."

Grandpa closed his eyes agin, this time for a long time. I reckoned I had tired him out too much and had ought to leave.

"I guess I better go, Grandpa. I love you."

He opened his eyes and took my hand and squoze it.

"I love you, too, boy. You take care of your ma, ye hear?"

"I will, Grandpa."

He closed his eyes agin and I snuck out.

MA HAD GOT us a hotel room what cost us seventy-five cents a day. There was only one bed and we slept together. She had brought food with us that lasted the day we came down and the next day. Then she bought a loaf of bread for nine cents and a quart of milk for eight, and that kept enough in our bellies for the day after that.

Grandpa passed on. I felt all sad and more'n a

little angry. I lost my grandpa just when I had found him—somebody who'd listen to me like I was growed and who could explain the world to me. But boys my age don't cry. Ma cried for half a day, then finished up makin' arrangements. We buried Grandpa and she cried some more. And then we took the bus back up home.

IT FELT good to get back and I was even glad to go to school. I got real busy catchin' up for a few days, but saw Harry when I walked Elliedine to school and back. Elliedine had got along right fine without me. The neighbor girl had walked with her the first day we was gone, but didn't bother after that. Harry done it. Didn't nobody ask him, but he saw she was alone and started walkin' with her. I thought that was just as fine as a split frog hair and I told Ma what he done. Harry went up about two notches on her importance stick from that.

THE NEXT DAY, I went over to Harry's after we got back from school.

"Ronson, we've missed two Sundays looking for the cadets at the churches. I didn't say anything, because I didn't want to discuss our plans in front of Elliedine. But we should get back to it."

"Yeah. We should," I said.

So, Sunday about a quarter to eleven, we were standin' with people outside the Episcopal church. We heard the sound of marchin' feet and shortly the Episcopal cadets were filing in. One and two and three ... and twelve and thirteen ... and ... bingo! There was Moley, sure as shootin'. The big dark mole on his cheek just in front of his ear. And his chin, what Harry called cleft.

I started to elbow Harry, but met his elbow halfway. He had seen him, too.

Seventeen ... eighteen .... and bingo agin. There was Whitey! We done lucked out. We looked over at the rows of cadets separated into companies and we could see which company they came from.

My heart was goin' a mile minute. I was so tickled, you wouldn't believe it. We kind of backed out through the folks outside the church 'til we was away from 'em and turned and started walkin'. We walked faster and faster 'til it turned into a run. We was so excited, we couldn't hold ourselves down. We run all the way to Harry's house. When we got there, we headed for our uprooted tree and we clumb to the highest branches what would take our weights. We started to laugh and we laughed harder and harder. Not cuz anything was funny, but just cuz we was feelin' so mighty. After we'd laughed ourselves silly and run out of feelin', I thought about it and talked to Harry.

"We ought to go and see Pete, Harry. We needs to ask him to find out the rest of what we gotta know."

And so we did.

WE WALKED OVER TO THE MANFREDS' house in town. It was a pretty long walk, cuz they lived on Draper Road past Airport Road. But we was in luck. When we got there, Pete was up on a ladder, cleaning snow out of the gutters. See, what happens is it would snow and then some warmer air would blow in and it would rain. Of course, the warmer rain would melt the snow, but sometimes it would take a day or two and in the meantime, with the gutters filled up, the rain would just run off like there wasn't no gutters. So folks tried to clean out the gutters before that happened. After about five minutes, Pete finished and climbed down. We come up to him. Harry knowed him better'n me, so I let Harry talk.

"Pete, we have identified the names and company of the cadets we told you about."

"OK," Pete said. "Write it down so I don't get it wrong and I'll check into it."

"Well, I gotta say, I don't like writin' stuff down what could be used to put us in trouble," I said.

"I get that, Ronson," Pete said. "That's good thinking. Just write down the two names and tell me the company designation. If somebody sees a scrap of paper with two first names written on it, they can't relate it to anything. I'll remember the company."

I felt some better, but wasn't real happy. Harry wrote down for him "Luther" and "Waylon."

"Wow!" Pete said. "They won't be hard to find. Those are pretty unusual names. Check with me tomorrow."

THE NEXT DAY, we walked over to Pete's house agin after school. Pete had come back from class.

"Hey, Harry, Ronson," he said. "That was easy. I wrote down the names and room numbers for you. Here." He handed Harry a sheet of paper.

"Luther Randolph," Harry read out.

"That's the dark-haired one," Pete said, "the one with the mole on his cheek and the deep cleft in his chin."

"Waylon Green," Harry read.

"And that's the light-haired one," Pete said.

I squinted my eyes, tryin' to stick it deep in my memory.

"Moley is Luther Randolph and Whitey is Waylon Green," I said out loud, and then said it agin to myself two or three times.

"Moley and Whitey!" Pete repeated. He grinned, then chuckled, then laughed.

"OK," Harry said, all excited. "We know their names and barracks room numbers."

Then he looked worried.

"But their room numbers are different. They're not roommates. And one is on the second floor and the other on the third floor."

I thought it through. We was gonna go in their rooms at night and throw a bucket of goop on them in bed. Which beds? It'd be awful if we missed the bad ones and doused their roommates.

"We need to know which beds they's in," I said.

"I don't see why you'd want that, and anyway you didn't ask me to get that," Pete said, "but you can find out easily enough. The bed assignments are posted with the names on the door frames. You can read it in the hallway."

"Why do they do that?" Harry asked.

"If a bed fails to meet make-up standards, the upperclassmen doing inspections need to know which cadet to blame and not to put it on his old lady," Pete answered.

"Old lady?" Harry and I asked, almost at the same time.

"That's what they call their roommate. It's been

a tradition for decades," Pete said. "The upperclassman will drop a quarter in the middle of the bed to see if it bounces. If it doesn't, the covers are not pulled tightly enough. They get demerits. And they'll wipe a white glove on the back of the bed frame or on the floor under the bed. If any dust shows up on the glove, they get demerits."

"When do they get time for studyin' with all the cleanin' and formations and demerit marchin' and stuff?" I asked Pete. I thought about how we got waked up of a mornin' by the bugle playin' reveille godawful early when the wind was from the northeast. Kids who lived on campus talked about how it was and we all knew their drill. The cadets had only a few minutes after reveille to make their beds and do their cleanin' and get their uniforms just right. The shirts had to be tucked in real tight without a wrinkle or a bulge or a fold showin'. Then they formed up all in perfect rows and columns and the cadet officers checked to see that everbody was there. Woe to the cadet who didn't show up on time for formation. Then they marched to breakfast.

Lordamercy! They marched everwhere. As if armies needed marchin' practice in nineteen and forty. If you was advancin' on enemies shootin' at you, was anybody seein' if your lines was all straight? And they marched to class and to lunch and to dinner. And at the end of the day, they formed up agin and marched to bed. We kids was put to sleep of a evenin' with the bugle playin' taps over at the barracks.

Well, Pete just shook his head at my question about them bein' too busy and said, "Ha!"

All of a sudden, I had a cold feelin' in my gizzard. S'pose we couldn't get into their rooms?

"Pete," I said, "do they lock their doors at night?"

"No. They're not allowed to. A cadet officer has to be able to enter at any time, day or night."

That should have made me feel better, but it didn't. My cold feelin' didn't go away.

BACK AT HARRY'S, I was feelin' all glum and scared.

"What's the matter, Ronson?" Harry asked.

"Think about how this'll work out, Harry. If we throw a bucket on a feller on the third floor, he's gonna start yellin' and his roommate and the cadets next door is all goin' to wake up. And with everbody yellin', the fellers on the second and first floors are goin' to wake up. It don't end with us throwin' the bucket. We got to get down to the second and then the first floor and get out before anybody can stop us. We'd be in deep slurry up to our peckers if they caught us."

"Oh. O-OH!" Harry said as the whole picture sunk in like butter on hot corn pone.

"And worse," I said, "they's on two floors. We gotta split up and each throw a bucket on different floors at the same time."

Harry hung his head like he does, but hung it lower'n I ever seen. He couldn't say nuthin', nuthin' at all.

We sat watchin' snow melt off the top of rocks as the sun snuck through and warmed the rock underneath. But our plan was all froze, and even Mister Sun couldn't melt that.

10

APRIL 1940

Ma wrote a letter to Miz Hillson thanking her for the telephone help so she could find out about Grandpa. She told Miz Hillson that Grandpa had passed on to meet his maker and that she been there to see him before he went only cuz Miz Hillson had been so kind. She took so long writin' that I knew she had a hard time with the letter. She never had no teachin' in how to write letters. I reckon she just gritted her teeth and done it as best she could, even knowin' it probably had mistakes in it. She sent me over with it. Miz Hillson opened it right then and when she read it, her eyes got all misty and I saw a couple of tears on her cheeks.

Then Miz Hillson made a chocolate cake with black frosting—I don't see how, but Harry said she mixed red, blue, and green food colorin' together—

and wrote "In Loving Memory" in white icing on it. She sent it over with Harry. Well, Ma just cried all over agin, but it was only half for Grandpa's goin'. The other half was for Miz Hillson bein' so nice to us. I just don't get why womenfolk cry when they's happy. Maybe that's why the books I been readin' from the 1800s say women is hys-teri-cal and weak. But ain't neither Ma or Miz Hillson weak. They's both strong folk.

We had the cake for dinner. After that, we each of us said a little prayer for Grandpa and we sung a hymn or two with Uncle Sedgwick pickin' his git-fiddle. That kind of put the lid on the jar for Grandpa's passin'. We was all able to get back to our chores.

Well, I think the Hillsons was even nicer to me than ever. I knowed Ma and Miz Hillson had respect for each other now and I think they respected my pa and Harry's pa, too. Miz Hillson knowed my pa was a strong, honest man what you could always count on, and Ma knowed that Doctor Hillson was always tryin' to help young folk get a better life.

ONE EVENIN' when the Hillsons was goin' to have a guest over, they invited me to stay. It turned out that he was hatchin' his edication under Doctor

Hillson's wing. He was what they called a Fellow, which means, far as I kin make out, a person what already got all his doctor edication but come back for more misery. It seemed like 'most everbody teachin' at the college was a doctor, but they was the kind of doctors who knew stuff, not the kind who fixed you when you was broken.

Their visitor's name was Arpad Pap. He come from a city name of Budapest in a country name of Hungary. Well, I couldn't see why they'd call it that name when folks had enough to eat. He certainly wasn't poor. He had on real fancy duds and talked very formal and highfalutin' like and held his cup of tea with his little finger stickin' out. I just stayed shut up and watched and listened. I never seen nuthin' like it before.

They talked about things I never heard of. It seems that Hungary had been head of a big empire earlier. There was a war buildin' up over in Europe. A Mister Horthy was regent of Hungary. He must have been sort of a king or somethin'. This Horthy was allyin' with Germany aginst Russia, or what they called the Soviets. To me that was the Reds. Doctor Pap said it was all the Red states like Yukrain and Bulgaria and such put together.

Then I heard somethin' I knowed about cuz I had read about it in the funny papers. It was about how Russia had attacked little Finland and Mister Roosevelt sent eight soldiers to show Russia he was against 'em. I remembered readin' how Flash Gordon had changed his century and come back to Earth from his planet Mongo to fight the Reds over invadin' Finland. Well, Doctor Pap said that suddenly the Reds swapped from bad to good and Mister Roosevelt was helpin' them against Germany. What had made Flash Gordon stop fightin' the Reds all of a sudden done fall into place in my mind with a click like a gate latch.

Flash was right in the middle of fightin' the mighty Red Sword, which Harry said was the Soviets, when he ups and sez he might have been wrong about the Red Sword and he gets in his spaceship and hightails it back to Mongo. He was so burnt he didn't never show his face on Earth agin. Now I could see what happened. America switched sides, which put Flash on the bad side, which must of burned the fingers of the feller what drawed the comic somethin' awful. The drawer feller jerked Flash out and sent him to where he had control over which side was good and which was bad and he could draw pictures of Flash without politics splashin' soup on his tie.

Then I had a thought—what they call a insight—what has stayed with me ever since. The more you know, the easier it is to know more. And I vowed I'd keep readin' and listenin' and learn more and more.

Well, it seems that America was now with

Russia against Germany and Hungary was with Germany against Russia, but neither America or Hungary was in the war right now, so it was OK for Doctor Pap to be here. It would make a body's head spin.

But then things lit up real interestin'. They got talkin' about wines and brandies and stuff what they called spirits and Doctor Hillson, he said he bet Doctor Pap couldn't tell where a certain spirit drink he had done come from. And Doctor Pap, he said he thinks he knows all the good whiskeys and brandies in the world, so he bet he could. It wasn't a money bet. It was just the loser had to admit he was wrong. That made it interestin', but nobody lost any money. I thought that was a good kind of bet.

Doctor Hillson goes in the kitchen and comes back with a fancy crystal goblet filled half up with his special drink. Doctor Pap tastes it, lettin' it sit on his tongue, then tastes it agin. It's clear he can't quite call it. Then he sets his goblet down and sits back and gives his decision, for all the world like a medical man tellin' you what's makin' you sick.

"It's definitely from Central Europe," he said. "It's not French or German or Italian."

"No, it's not," said Doctor Hillson.

"And no one in Eastern Europe makes so fine a whiskey. And it's not Hungarian, either. I can't call the vineyard, but I'll wager it's Czech."

"Not quite," said Doctor Hillson, with a sneaky little grin on his face.

"May I see the bottle, please?" Doctor Pap asked.

"I'll fetch the container," said Doctor Hillson. I could see he needed to laugh but was holdin' his face as straight as a old woman in a corset. He went out to the kitchen and come back holdin'—I could hardly believe it—a stone jug of moonshine!

"It was made here in the wilds of Appalachia," he said. "I had a student, a local boy from the hills between here and Kentucky. That's the next state, due west from us. He wasn't doing well. I gave him a little extra tutoring, but he just couldn't comprehend. Toward the end of the quarter, it became clear that he wasn't going to pass. Then one day, at about 11:55 after I had concluded an 11 o'clock class and was finishing with student questions, he asked me what time I went to lunch. 'About noon,' I told him, 'as soon as I finish with these students.' I didn't understand the reason for his question. He just turned and left. When I got back from lunch, this jug was sitting on my desk, no note, no message. He'd asked just so I'd know who it was from, but without any sort of traceable commitment. Clearly it was a bribe."

Doctor Pap picked up his goblet.

"This came from that?" he asked, liftin' his goblet and pointin' at the jug, like he didn't believe it any mor'n he'd believe hogs could sprout wings and fly.

"Yes, it did," Doctor Hillson said. "Most moonshine, also often called 'white lightning,' is made in a way we might call 'quick and dirty,' rather literally, because it might be made in a month and you might find foreign objects, like snake skeletons, in the mash. But the occasional maker starts with high quality materials, uses sanitary procedures, and ages it in burned-out oak casks for years. This one, I think, was aged several years. It is possible to make a fine drink, as you have experienced."

Doctor Pap done laughed at bein' taken in, playin' like he wasn't bothered by bein' honeyfuggled. And mebbe he wasn't. He had one question.

"To write *finis* to your engaging story," he said, "tell us if the student passed."

"Well," answered Doctor Hillson, "he received the D he deserved. I tried to give the jug back, but he denied knowing anything about it."

Well, I was as tickled as a dog what had got a beefsteak. I could hardly keep from laughin' out loud. Doctor Hillson had won the bet big. But he didn't want to rub it in, so he started askin' Doctor Pap about things over in Hungary. One story led to another until Doctor Pap, he told about facin' some wolves. It perked up my ears 'til they must have looked like those on the wolves.

"My family has a cabin in the forest near Budapest where we vacation. One winter day, I was hiking nearby the cabin when a pack of wolves approached me. There were eight. Big beasts and hungry. I leapt for the nearest tree and was out of their reach before they recovered from their surprise and came for me. They were growling and leaping. I always carried a handgun, my Beretta model 1934 with seven shots. It was a nine-millimeter, a heavy enough caliber to kill a wolf. But, even assuming I didn't miss, I didn't have enough bullets. I waited some time, but the wolves waited as well. It became clear they were not going away. And when night came, I would either freeze to death or fall asleep and fall out of the tree into their midst. I couldn't see a solution."

He paused. I was thinkin' he'd told this story before and knowed when to pause to get everbody worked up. Doctor Hillson didn't say nuthin'. I guess he didn't want to feel controlled. But Miz Hillson was just caught up in the story.

"So what did you do, Arpad?" she asked.

"What do I do when I cannot think of a solution to a problem? Think deeper and wider. My only course of action was to shoot eight of them with seven shots. They were moving around somewhat. I waited until I thought two were lined up, aimed carefully, and fired. One went down, but the bullet missed the other. I tried again, killed another, but only one. This wasn't going to work. I was looking down on them and one would not be above another. I had to get them jumping. I climbed partway down and lowered a foot within their reach, then withdrew it quickly. They started jumping up, trying to grab the foot. When I thought two were lined up, I fired my third and then my fourth bullets. Two single hits. But on the fifth, it got the highest jumper and passed on to another below. The second one was only wounded, but it 'yip-yipped' and slunk away limping. Now there were two shots and two wolves. You can imagine how carefully I aimed. I don't think all seven on the ground were dead, but at least they were too badly wounded to go after me. I watched for a few minutes, then dropped to the ground and started running. I'll bet I would have won an Olympic dash. I have never been so frightened before or since. I slept with my pistol under my pillow until we got back to Budapest."

He sat back, showin' he done finished his story. Everbody sat quiet for a couple minutes, enjoyin' the pictures the story put in our minds. Then Miz Hillson said it was time for the boys to go to bed and I went home.

But I didn't sleep good that night. I thought about what Doctor Pap had said. When you can't solve a problem, think deeper and wider. That's what Harry and I gotta do. If he could outsmart those wolves, Harry and I could outsmart our coyote cadets.

THE NEXT DAY, I TOL' Harry what I was thinkin'. He got all excited and we started plannin' ways to do our job. I put the deeper and wider together with what Elliedine had said—a step at a time. First we gotta get in place, then throw our buckets, and finally get out without bein' caught. We gotta time it all just exact. Harry's got a watch what got a second hand, so we can get it timed down to the second. And to do that, we gotta practice over and over like the ball players practice in Miles Stadium before they has a game.

"We have to get in quietly and in the dark so nobody hears us or sees us," Harry said.

"We could wear tennis shoes. They would make us as quiet as a mouse."

"Great. And they have good traction. We could wear dark clothes and move with no light. We could count the number of steps, get close, and feel our way the last two or three feet. One quick flash to make a final verification. That makes the only light as one second of a hooded flashlight just a second or two before the act."

"We gotta borrow a couple of flashlights. I ain't got none."

"We have one at my house I can take. But we have to find another one."

"Countin' steps and all means we'd have to go beforehand when nobody's there and practice 'til we can walk in with our eyes closed."

Harry closed his eyes real tight and almost shook. It made me think of a wet dog. Maybe he was fightin' his fear. Then he opened his eyes and stood up real straight. "We can do that."

"OK. That gets us in. Then we gotta practice throwin' buckets. We'd use the buckets we's gonna use in the real thing, so as to get the feel. We could use the stump of our uprooted tree. That about the length and height of Moley or Whitey lyin' in a bunk. We fill the bucket with water and practice liftin' it and aimin' it and throwin' it, over and over 'til we get it right."

"Right," Harry agreed. "That gets us through the second step. Then we have to work out how we get out safely. How are we going to leave the scene after we're out of the barracks when the locals are pouring out after us with their torches and pitchforks?"

"Wha-a-at?" I said. "What in tarnation is you talkin' about, Harry?"

"Oh, never mind," he said. "It's just from a book by Mary Shelley. Forget it."

"Oh, yessiree, I'll do that," I said. "Faster'n a fox after a rabbit."

"But we have to figure how to escape, Ronson. That's paramount."

I shook my head. I could read books from here to glory, but I'd never catch up with Harry's words, cuz he'd be readin', too. Oh, well …

"Let's look at it abstractly," Harry said. "Men are running. How do we stop them?"

"A wire across the doorway."

"Oh, be real. If we put it up in advance, it would deter us. And they might find it and be warned. If we didn't put it up in advance, how are we going to take time to hook it when they're after us?"

Well, I had to admit that Harry was thinkin' pretty good now. I made a picture in my mind of cadets runnin' out of their rooms in their peejammies.

"Gravel," I said. "They's barefoot. We sprinkle gravel behind us as we run. They'd slow down trying t' run barefoot over gravel."

Harry's eyes lit up.

"No, Ronson. Better: tacks. We sprinkle thumbtacks behind us as we run."

The picture in my mind done turn just beautiful.

"Oh my, oh my!" I said. "Yeah. You got it. If a feller gets a tack or two in his foot, he ain't goin' to run no more or even take one step 'til he pulls it out."

Well, I tell you! We was very tickled with

ourselves. We each carry a box of tacks and we just sprinkle them behind us as we run. It don't take no time or slow us down, and ain't nobody barefoot gonna get past our carpet of tacks.

We's getting there. What looked like a mountain we couldn't climb was now shrunk to just a hill, thanks to Doctor Pap and Elliedine—and it was gettin' smaller with each idea.

ON SUNDAY when we didn't have school and all the cadets had been marched to church, we went to the section of barracks where Moley and Whitey was holin' up. These barracks, across the street from the drill field, was pretty new, not like the old ones on the hill above College Avenue. They was made of stone. When we went inside, we seen they had cement stairs and tile floors. It was all good for us. No boards to squeak or give us splinters.

We was ever so nervous. Suppose they had a guard what made rounds. Or a cadet who was sick that day and stayed in bed? If anybody even saw us, they would be warned. We did everthing quick as a fox runnin' from a hound.

We got the layout in our minds, the brush and trees outside, the sidewalks and paths leadin' to it from all directions and where the stairs and their rooms was. All the doors was open and we could see which beds was theirs.

I had a mind to mess up their beds so they'd get de-merits, but, thinkin' about it, they'd know somebody'd been there. Better nobody gets a hint of us 'til the big event.

Harry timed us sneakin' in, goin' through motions, and runnin' out. He wrote down the time for each step. Then we made like we was the roommate or a cadet from another room gettin' waked up and runnin' out and we timed that.

It was about time for the cadets to come marchin' back, so we snuck out and went back to Harry's. We went up in the playhouse to the upper floor and put our heads together to see how far we'd got.

Harry added up the times for each step and got the time from beginnin' to end. We agreed that I'd take the third floor and he'd take the second, cuz I was faster at runnin'.

"We got a problem, Harry," I said. "If we does it at the same time, the cadets on the second floor will be comin' out as I'm runnin' down and I can't sprinkle tacks 'til you has gone by."

"That's right," he said. He frowned and stroked his chin like we seen the detectives do in the movies. "You have to do it first, then just as you get to the bottom of the stairwell, I do it. Then we're together and run out leaving the tacks."

"We needs a signal. I can make a owl hoot just before I throw the bucket. We know the time it takes for me to get down. You count the seconds after the owl hoot and then you throw your bucket."

"Suppose there's a real owl throwing our timing off."

"There ain't no real owls in those barracks," I said. "They's new."

Harry looked at the list of times agin.

"That would work," he said at last. But then he looked all serious like and dropped the next bomb on our plans.

"That takes care of the third and second floors, Ronson, but not the first. If there's enough clamor from above, the guys on the first floor will be coming out just as we're running past. One or another of them would be alert enough to catch us."

I didn't know what to say. He was right. If Moley and Whitey had been on the first and second floors, we'd be munchin' clover. But this was bad. We thought and thought, but got nuthin' thunk. We went through the steps and times agin and agin, but it come out the same every time. All our plans was about as much use as tits on a boar hog. We done give up for the day and went home.

THAT NIGHT, I WAS LYIN' awake, worryin'. I couldn't sleep for nuthin'. I thought through what Doctor Pap had said. I pictured it in my mind. He had to get two wolves with one shot, so he had to make them line up. Then I pictured the cadets comin' out of their rooms. We had to make them stop. What would stop them? We couldn't block off all the doors. I thought mebbe if I could borrow a pistol, I could shoot a blank and they'd be too scared to come out. But these fellers is trainin' for war. At least some wouldn't be scared. And where could I get a pistol anyways?

Then I thought, well, we stopped the fellers runnin' after us with tacks. And it hit me upside the head. If tacks could stop folks from runnin', it could keep them from startin' to run. My mind what had been all spinnin' around like a airyplane propeller done slowed and stopped. I felt kind of peaceful like. And I went to sleep.

THE NEXT DAY, Harry and I was walkin' to school. I could hardly wait to tell him my idea.

"I think I got the answer to the first-floor cadets, Harry."

He waited a minute for me to go on, but I didn't. I wanted to stretch out the good feelin' I got.

"Well? What?"

"When we're goin' in, we sprinkle tacks in front of every door on the first floor. But not in the middle of the hall where we gotta run out. Then if somebody starts to come out, they'll stop, sure as shootin'."

Harry started wavin' his arms. I thought he was tryin' to fly. He whooped and nodded and looked at me with his eyes all shiny.

"That's it, Ronson. You got it. Marvelous!"

And we both glowed all the way to school.

"Now let's plan the second step," Harry said when we was home after school.

"We can borrow two buckets from the barns," I said. "They got so many, they won't miss a couple for one night. And they got some with lids hinged to 'em so's we can close off the stink from the skunk spray 'til we's ready to throw."

"Mrs. Skunk, will you please spray some of your scent into our buckets but not on us? There's a good girl," Harry said, all sarcastic.

"Yeah, I see what you mean. Ain't no way we kin get skunk spray. But the slurry from the floor of the barn stinks almost as bad and it stains whatever it touches, and ye has to wash somethin' three or four times to get the smell out."

"Ooh! Great idea, Ronson, we'll use slurry. It's easy to get."

"And we kin take a leak in the pails to make it a little thinner if it needs it."

Harry sniggered.

So we snuck two pails with lids and filled 'em with water and practiced carryin' 'em and heftin' 'em and throwin' the water on the tree roots 'til it got all easy.

"Now for the third step," I said. "What do we need for that?"

"Tacks," Harry said. "Lots of tacks. We can't borrow those anywhere. We need money to buy tacks."

"How much?" I asked.

"That depends on how many we need."

"We got to spread them thick enough that ain't nobody gonna miss them just by luck and be able to come after us. I reckon that means a tack at least every two inches. And we can't set 'em in a row. We gotta dump 'em and they's gonna fall ever whichee way."

"Not dump. At least we can dribble them across a doorway," Harry said, "so there are more in the width dimension than the depth dimension."

I didn't get all his words, but he was holdin' his

hands in shapes as he talked, so I got the picture. I got a handful of pebbles and dropped them in a clear spot of earth and we counted them.

"It looks like we need about three dozen per door for the first floor," Harry calculated. "With sixteen doors, that's about 550 tacks just for that."

I sighed. That was a lot. "And when I run down the stairs from the third to the second floor, I can sprinkle tacks on the landin' where the stairs turn and go in the other direction. Anyone followin' us has to go across that. It's about four foot by four foot. If we make a two-foot-wide patch of tacks four foot across, that ought to do it."

We looked at the sprinkle of pebbles and multiplied. I never figured I'd use my times tables in real life, but here I was needin' it.

"Looks like about five hundred," Harry said.

"Yeah," I agreed, "That's about right."

"Doing the same on the next landing is five hundred more. That totals to about fifteen hundred tacks," Harry said.

"How much would that cost?"

"No idea."

We went to Roses Five and Dime store. We didn't ask, cuz we didn't want nobody to connect us with tack buyin'. We looked. There was a case of ten boxes, fifty tacks a box, comin' to five hundred tacks a case for thirty-five cents. We needed three cases.

"That's more'n a dollar, Harry!"

"A dollar five."

And we walked out.

"Where are we gonna get that kind of money, Harry?"

"I have over forty cents saved up."

"I ain't got nuthin'."

"We'll have to get some kind of job."

"And if we do buy them," I said, "we can't buy them all at once. It'd be a big buy and the salesgirl would likely remember us."

"You're right, Ronson. One of us will buy the first case. A week later, the other will buy the second. And in still another week, we'll wait until there's a different salesgirl on duty and buy the third."

"OK, Harry, but we ain't got the money."

And there it sat.

11

MAY 1940

Me an' Harry couldn't find no jobs. We was too young for anybody to take us serious-like. But one day, a piece of luck hit. Well, luck for us, not for Mac. Mac Holdaway, who was a little older than we was, had a job cuttin' the grass for some neighbors, the Masseys. They paid him a whole quarter for doin' the entire yard, which was pretty big.

One week Mac got the flu or somethin' and couldn't do it and asked Harry if he'd fill in. 'Course Harry said he would and he asked me to help, since it were a big job. We went over Saturday and took turns pushin' that little mowing machine back and forth clippety-clip over the grass, up a row and back the next row and back agin, for hours. It was warm and we was sweatin' and tired, even though we traded off doin' it. Harry got all red-faced and dizzy once and I sat him in the shade of a tree. I figgered he was gettin' what they call dehydrapated. I borrowed a cup from Miz Massey and filled it from a hose and give him it. He got better real fast and was soon takin' his turn agin.

Well, we got it done and we got the quarter for it. What with the forty cents he already had, that made sixty-five cents. We was lackin' just forty cents now to be able to buy the tacks.

We was in the middle of baseball season and we'd been doin' the batboy job agin. At the end of one of the games, Harry and I was walkin' out of the stadium when we come across a drunk feller. A lot of folks who had been students like to come back and watch the sports playin'. Well, sometimes fellers what is away from their wives get together and start on the moonshine—or maybe Kentucky whiskey—and they don't know when to quit. And here we come across such a feller what had had too much. He didn't know where he was or was goin'. He was havin' trouble enough just standin' up and walkin'. I feel right sorry for a feller in that condition. It's like the drink just snuck up and took away his judgment before he knowed it. I mean, I seen Uncle Sedg like that a time or two. Harry and I offered to help this feller.

"I gotta find my car. Don't know where ...," he said.

"You can't drive like that. You'll kill yerself," I said.

"Don't wanna drive. Gotta sleep," he said, hardly able to get the words out.

"What kind of car do you have?" Harry asked.

"Studebaker, 1938," he mumbled. "Dark blue."

We took him to the parking row around the edge of the stadium—they had room for a few cars there. We figgered he wouldn't be lookin' for his car up here if he'd left it in town or down on campus, so most likely it'd be around here.

We walked one on each side of him, half holdin' him up, past the row of cars 'til we come on a Studebaker.

"Is that it?" I asked.

"Naw. Thass ... wrong ... wrong ... color," he got out. He hiccupped. I was afraid he was gonna puke on us, but he didn't. In the next row, we come to a dark blue Studebaker.

"Is that it?" I asked agin.

"Thass ... thass ...," he said, not bein' able to finish.

"Key," Harry said. "If your key fits, it's yours."

"Pocket," he said. We started goin' through his pockets. He just stood there, peaceful like, his head bobblin' back and forth.

"Got it," Harry said and let go of him to try the

key. The feller almost fell down, but I managed to hold him.

"It fits," Harry said and opened the door.

"Thank you ... thank you so much ... boys," he mumbled and lurched to the car. "Here," he said, reaching in his pocket. He pulled out a coin and slipped it into my hand and almost fell into the car. He crawled the rest of the way in, lying on the seat. Harry reached in, put the key into the ignition, and shut the door. Our drunk was dead asleep already.

I looked at the coin.

"Fifty cents, Harry! It's a fifty-cent piece! We got enough for the tacks now," I chortled. We looked at the coin and there was Miss Liberty walkin' along in front of the risin' sun. We was so excited, we ran all the way home.

THE NEXT DAY I went to the five and dime and bought a case of tacks. I noted it was a salesgirl with a name tag "Susan" who waited on me. A week later, Harry went. Susan agin. Then I started lookin' in each day to see who was on duty. Susan, Susan, Susan. Then it were Abigail. I went in and bought the third case. We now had all the tacks and no one had bought enough for a clerk to remember.

"This is some humongous bunch of tacks," I

said. "We can't carry cases of them and be openin' boxes when we're spreadin' 'em."

"Yes, you're right. We each need a holder for a case-and-a-half worth that will dispense them at the right rate."

I looked down at my feet and scratched my head. "A box is too big and unhandy. A soft bag would let the tacks get caught up in the fabric."

"We need something with a stiff surface but still somewhat flexible. And that we can hold in one hand," Harry said. "Like a stiff bag. But I don't know where we'd find something like that."

"Then we has to get ordinary bags and make them stiff."

"Right. That might work." Harry stared into the distance, thinkin'. "I think I have it. My mom buys vegetables in cloth sacks. They come in different sizes, by what's in 'em. If we super-starched them, they'd be pretty stiff."

He went home and come back with a couple of bags the right size and a box of starch. We ran them through starching over and over until they was stiff. Then we tried tacks in them. It worked. The tacks didn't hang up and they poured out when we tipped the bag—and we could hold it with one hand. We adjusted the drawstring at the opening until the tacks came out about the speed we wanted. Then we practiced until we could dump tacks spread out the way we wanted left-handed in a marked-off space. One more thing was ready.

THE NEXT EVENIN', Harry said to me, "We have to get on with it. It's well into May. In another couple of weeks, they'll start studying for exams, then exams begin. Times get irregular and we can't count on our plan. Then summer break. We don't know if they'll come back next year and, if they do, they'll be in different barrack rooms. We'd have to start all over."

I felt cold inside, scared. But Harry was right. It'd been over half a year since they hurt Elliedine and we hadn't done nuthin'. If we waited, it'd be too late. I sighed a big sigh.

"Yeah, Harry, yer right. We gotta do it this week or next."

"How can we decide what night to pick?"

"It'd help on our gettin' in and out and seein' bed outlines if we had a bright moon," I said.

We went out and looked at the sky. The sun hadn't set yet, bein' May, but I could see a faint moon. It showed half.

"Is it gettin' bigger or smaller?" I asked.

"And will it be cloudy?" Harry asked.

He went in his house and got the *Roanoke Times* and looked up the weather.

"It's getting bigger. That means it'll be gibbous to full next week and the forecast is for clear skies on Tuesday, Wednesday, and Thursday," Harry said.

"That's it, then. Middle of next week," I said.

"I'm scared, Ronson." Most boys wouldn't admit to that. But Harry and I had grown up bein' close. And we'd got real open with each other's thinkin' while we was plannin' this thing. He told me stuff honest-like and then I told him honest-like.

"Me, too, Harry. But every time we feel scared, we gotta remember Elliedine and how sad and hurt she was. We's doin' it for Ellie, not for us."

"How're we going to get away after we get out of the barracks?" Harry asked.

"We can't hide. They might gather around and wait 'til light. We gotta keep movin' away."

"We don't have a car, so our choices are running or bicycling," Harry said.

"Seem like, t'me, while it's faster, a bicycle keeps us on roads or walkways, easy to see, easy to stop. And carryin' our stuff, buckets and flashlights, would be hard on a bike. On foot, we kin hide in a shadow, then move farther. We kin go in any direction."

Harry thought, noddin' this way and that, then looked at me, his mouth pushed tight in a straight line.

"I guess," he agreed.

"Then on Sunday, we go and do a final practice and at the end, do a getaway practice."

"I think we should each go a different way," he said. "Then they wouldn't know who to follow and it would split them up."

"They's bigger'n we is, Harry. It wouldn't take but one to catch one of us. And goin' two directions doubles the chance they gets one of us. And if they gets one, they gets t'other."

"I suppose, Ronson. I suppose. Which way do you think we should head?"

"Well, toward town, toward the duck pond, or out on the drill field puts us in the open. They'd see us. We have to go up the rise in the back where there are trees and bushes to hide in. Either toward the stadium or to the right or left of it. They won't know whichaway we went and the farther we get, the bigger the area they'd have to search."

"Suppose one of them gets a look at our faces," Harry said. "He might recognize us later."

"Oh-oh! Yer right, Harry. We'z got to mask up like the bank robbers in the western movies."

We didn't have big bandanas like them bank robbers, so we made do with smaller masks. We got handkerchiefs, rolled the corners into little twists, and tied them onto string. We made a loop of string on each side and fit the loop over our ears. It not only covered up most of our faces, but it changed the shape somebody would see from the side. We dug out winter stockin' caps. They would cover up our hair and change the shape of our heads.

"This is good," Harry said. "No one can discern any features but our eyes. And it will be night."

"I agree. Now all we got to do is get our movements to where we can do them without thinkin'. Sunday, when the cadets are at church and we do our next practice, we'll also practice a getaway."

ON SATURDAY, we went back to Pete's house. He'd been helpin' us, so we figgered we could trust him. We told him the truth about why we was doin' it. He allowed it was somethin' what oughta be done to them fellers and agreed to not tell anyone about Elliedine. We told him what our plans was. He went over it with us step-by-step. When we got to goin' in the barracks rooms, he said we could borrow his flashlight and he got it for us. So now we had the two.

"One thing bothers me about this," he said. "Will they know why it's being done? Your whole purpose is to punish them. If they don't know why, it's just a bad experience, not a punishment."

Well, we never thought of that. We was so hung up on the how that we never thought about the why. We looked at each other and I was sure Harry was thinkin' the same thing I was—how could we be so dumb.

And then my train of thoughts done got to another station, all huffin' and blowin' smoke inside my mind. If we hadn't thought of that, what else hadn't we thought of? I felt scared all over agin.

Harry picked the question up.

"How can we do that, Pete?" he asked.

"You each drop a note just inside the door a little to the side," he said. "Written in big block letters so they can't trace the handwriting and written with a pencil anyone could have on paper you can buy at any store. Nothing even experts could trace."

"Yeah," I said, "that wut'n take no more time if we had them all writ up beforehand."

"What do we say?" Harry asked. "Do we write 'This is payback for hurting Elliedine'?"

"Don't use her name. They probably don't know it and it would make anyone think that family had done it," said Pete.

"They's gonna think that anyways," I said.

"They will suspect it, but you want to leave as much room for other interpretations as possible. If they went to the law, they'd have to have evidence beyond a reasonable doubt, so you want to insert all the doubt you can. I'll help you word it," added Pete.

"We're ever so indebted to you, Pete," Harry said. "We couldn't have gotten this far without your help."

"I'd like to see justice done, too, Harry," he said. "Those two are a mean pair of suckers."

He went to get a paper and pencil. When he come back, he spoke out another thought.

"You know what would make it even stronger? If you said you plan to get at them farther in the future. Make them worry. Make them look over their shoulders, metaphorically speaking, forever after."

"That's a marvelous idea," Harry said.

And Pete started to write.

THIS IS FOR THE 15-YEAR-OLD GIRL YOU RAPED LAST FALL. WE KNOW WHO YOU ARE. WE WILL COME BACK.

"You see," Pete said after we had read it, "they can't show this to anybody without admitting they're accused of rape. They won't risk taking the note to the authorities."

"Clever, clever," Harry said.

I just shook my head. Pete was so far ahead of us, I didn't know what to say.

THE NEXT DAY, while the cadets was at church, we practiced for the last time. We walked into the first floor and made like we was spreadin' tacks in front of each door, Harry on one side of the hall and me on t'other. Then we went up the stairs to the second floor. Harry walked down toward Whitey's room while I went up to the third. I walked down to Moley's room, made like gettin' out my note and my tacks, and made my owl hoot for Harry to start countin' seconds. I stepped in and made like I dropped the note and chucked the bucket at his bed. Then I ran out and back to the stairs, makin' like I was sprinklin' tacks behind me on the stairs landing. Just as I got down to the second level, here come Harry, runnin' and makin' like he was sprinklin' tacks. He followed me to the first floor and we run for the door. We run down the side of the building to its back and across the walk and up the rise into the bushes. We headed up the hill toward the right and then, when we was out of sight of the sidewalk below, switched our direction to go left. We went up through the college's tree nursery to Clay Street and headed toward town. After a block past the college's pillar marks, we figgered we could go left or straight or right or even catty-wampus across the open field and nobody'd know which way we went. We stopped and caught our breath.

"It looks good to me," Harry said. "I think we're OK."

I nodded. We shook hands and grinned and walked back home.

We set for Tuesday, but it were cloudy. Wednesday was clear and the moon was close to full, so that was it. Harry and I was both as nervous as a coon in a bear's den. I didn't know if I could pull it off when it was for real. I kept thinkin' of how Elliedine didn't smile that purty smile of hers no more and it got me riled up enough to forget my worries. I don't know how Harry did it, but he must've done somethin' like that, cuz he didn't back out.

I told my folks I was goin' to sleep over to Harry's, cuz I was in the one room together with all my fambly and I couldn't be sure of sneakin' out and back in. Harry told his folks we was goin' to practice camping out for a Boy Scout merit badge. He had a sleepin' bag and borrowed his pa's for me.

We cleared a spot in the woods just across the fence from his folks' house and set up our bags and stuff. Harry had squirreled away some food to add to the buckets of slurry a long time ago in his hidey-hole in the playhouse, so we had a couple of rotten eggs and some rotten tomatoes and vegetables. We had hid our notes we made in there, too. After dinner and before it got dark, we snuck up to the barns and looked for buckets. We took two empty ones with hinged lids and carryin' straps that went over our shoulders to carry them when they were heavy. We filled our buckets about two-thirds up with the stinkingest slurry we could find. We come back and added the eggs and tomatoes and stuff. Then we took pisses, each in one of the buckets. They was filled almost to the top. I was awful glad we had lids for 'em, cuz the stink was somethin' awful. It was gettin' dark then. Harry set his alarm clock for 1:00 and we lay down to sleep.

Sleep? I began to wonder what that was. I was just too nervous to even hold still. I could hear Harry threshin' around, too. I guess I must of drifted off, cuz the alarm rang and I jumped like I had stepped on a snake.

We got up and picked up our tacks and notes and flashlights and buckets before we was awake enough to think about it. Then it hit us what we was about to do. We both stopped and stood still, lookin' at each other in the moonlight. I could see Harry was as scared as I was.

"Just think about Ellie," I said. "Every time you start to worry, picture them hurtin' her in yer mind."

"Yeah," Harry said. "OK."

And we started off.

WITH OUR EYES adjusted to the dark, the moon lighted the way almost like daylight. The buckets was heavy and we kept shiftin' them from one hand to t'other.

I heard Harry whisperin' to hisself, "If I can keep in mind what Elliedine went through, I can get through this."

I thought of my sweet gentle sister bein' jumped by these two animals and I kept my mad up enough that I didn't think so much of how scared I was.

We got there and stopped outside the barracks.

"Now we don't think about anything but what we practiced," I told Harry in a low voice. "We think only about the step we's doin' at that moment and then the next step. Nuthin' else."

"OK, Ronson," Harry replied.

I looked over and saw Harry was walking stiff like a ironing board. His head was pulled back and I could see folds of skin in wrinkles around his neck.

"Relax, Harry. Ye can't move right when you're stiff like that."

He stopped and wilted like a flower in a hot oven.

"You relax yourself, Ronson," he hissed.

I done stop to feel myself and, sure as rain on a picnic, I was all stiff, too. I made myself droop and rolled my head around in a circle and jerked my shoulders up and down.

We looked at each other and laughed. We settled down a peg and we was walkin' normal agin.

Then I had a thought.

"Let's don't say our names, just in case someone might hear us. I'm gettin' Moley and you's gettin' Whitey, so call me Moley and I'll call you Whitey."

"Good idea, Moley," Harry said.

"C'mon, Whitey, let's do it before we has time to think about it."

We put on our masks and knit hats and walked into the barracks.

THE MOONLIGHT WAS bright enough from the door and stairwell windows to see where we was goin' without usin' the flashlights. We started spreadin' tacks in front of the doors like we planned. I heard a voice from one of the rooms. My heart jumped up in my throat and I could hardly swallow it back down. Then the voice turn to snores. Just one of the cadets dreamin', I guessed. We went on.

We got to the stairwell at the end of the hall and started up. Harry was shakin' so bad his bucket slop was hittin' the lid and dribblin' out. I could smell it. *Oh, God.* I started shakin', too. *I gotta stop this.*

"For Ellie," I said out loud. It were a risk, but better'n blowin' the whole shebang.

Harry calmed down a little and we climbed to the second floor. I whacked him on the shoulder. He straightened up tall and turned to walk down the hallway. I climbed on to the third floor.

We was alone with it, now. In a way it was better, cuz I didn't feel I had to buck Harry up. But if he didn't do his part right, we'd be in deep slurry ourselves. I couldn't think about that. I was all sweat on my face. I wiped my sleeve over my forehead. I felt both hot and cold all over at the same time. I wondered if this was like what Pa felt when he was goin' into battle in the Great War. Well, he was facin' death, I told myself. I was just facin' a crew of angry cadets. If he could fight the war, I could do my job for Elliedine.

I walked down the hall to Moley's room, countin' the steps like we practiced. There it was. The door. I got my tacks ready to sprinkle behind me and my note ready to drop and took the lid off the bucket and got my flashlight ready to aim. I reached for the doorknob and started to turn it. Then I remembered. I stopped and made my owl hoot. Harry hooted back—he'd heard me.

I reached for the knob agin and just froze. I couldn't move. But Harry was countin' down. If I didn't do it, he'd be doin' it and droppin' tacks and I'd be stuck up here cut off in the middle of a whole company of cadets. I was breathin' a mile a minute. My eyes was seein' and blindin' and seein' and blindin' back and forth. Finally, the fear of bein' caught up here got bigger'n my freeze.

I grabbed the knob, turned it, and pushed the door open. A quick flash showed just where Moley's bed was. I was holdin' the bucket handle in my left hand with the flashlight under my thumb. I reached my arm out to the side and dropped my note with my right hand. Then I grabbed the bottom of the bucket with it. I hefted the bucket and threw its innerds right on Moley. I turned and was out the door faster'n Flash Gordon's spaceship. I heard Moley scream as I ran and a second later other cadets wakin' up and sayin' "What?" and "What the hell?"

I reached the stairwell and almost jumped down to the landin' at the middle, my feet hardly touchin' the stairs. I sprinkled tacks on the landin', like we'd planned, and almost jumped agin down to the bottom. I heard yells and curses from down the second-floor hallway and here come Harry, lickety-split. I had lost a couple of seconds with my freeze, but made it up with my stair jumps. I seen his face above his mask was white as a ghost, even in the reflected moonlight.

I heard a whole passel of screams from the third-floor stairwell. The cadets must have been makin' the acquaintance of my tacks.

I went on down to the first floor, jumpin' like before. Harry stopped to spread his tacks, so I was about eight or ten steps ahead of him. The first-floor cadets had been waked up by the ruckus and yellin' and they was openin' their doors, lookin' out to see what was goin' on. A couple started to step out, but met the tacks and started screamin' bloody murder.

Well, one cadet must have been more awake than the others. He was so big I'd bet he was a football player. He seen us runnin' from the yellin' and he turned on his light and seen the tacks. He jumped over them just as I reached him. He was a little off balance from his jump, landin' up against the opposite wall. I swung my bucket backwards and hit him in the back of the head. It didn't do him any big harm, a empty bucket, but throwed him off balance agin. I turned and ran.

Harry was just comin' up. The cadet was on his hands and knees, but grabbed Harry's ankle as he was runnin' by. Harry was stopped. *Hit him, Harry,* I thought. But he didn't. He just stood there like a scared rabbit freezin' up before a wolf. I was close to panickin'. I hit the cadet's arm that was holdin' Harry with my bucket. He dropped his grip. I pulled Harry on and yelled "Run!" He ran. I was hot on his heels. But the cadet had got up and was after us.

We didn't have time to get to the brush. He was bigger and faster than we was and he was catchin' up to us. My heart went from thump to thunder. I felt somehow like water was runnin' down my neck and back. I ain't had that feelin' since a angry bull come at me when I was fifty yards from a fence. If he got us, we was finished.

I thought, *if I'm losin' cuz he's bigger'n me, I gotta use my bein' smaller to get us away.*

It hit me what to do. Just before he got to me, I stopped runnin' and squatted and curled up as small as I could get. He was goin' too fast to stop. He fell over me and sprawled all spread-eagled on the ground. Well, this time I swung my bucket as hard as I could right into the back of his head. He started gettin' up, although pretty slow. I ran after Harry and we got into the brush while the cadet was still tryin' to stand straight. There wasn't no others comin' out of the barracks, they all bein' busy pullin' tacks out'n their feet.

From the sidewalk outside the barracks' entrance, scrub bushes about three or four feet high were growin' all the way up the hill. We ducked into the scrub, squattin' down and sort of duck-waddlin' between the bush trunks. This kept the tops of the plants over our heads. I s'pose we made them wiggle a bit, but there was a breeze movin' others and it was night. No one could tell by moonlight where we was scootin'.

Harry and I did what we'd practiced—headin' one way while any followers could see where we was headin' and then, when we was out of sight, turnin' and goin' the other. We run and we run. The bushes was hittin' us all over, flappin' against our faces, but they was all baby plants an' they didn't scratch us or slow us down.

About halfway up the hill, I stopped and looked back between the branches of a little tree. A bright light was shinin' over the door to the barracks. Cadets was pouring from the door as thick as bats out'n a cave at sunset. For a second, I was afraid they'd hear us pantin' hard, but they was all yellin' and pantin' themselves, louder than we was. We pulled our masks off so we could breathe better and stuffed them in our pockets. We didn't want to leave any trace of our bein' there. I gave Harry a push to start him and we ran even faster than before, payin' no mind to the branches that brushed us as we went past.

When we got through the plant nursery to Clay Street, we didn't have breath to run no more. We stopped. Our chests was heavin' in and out.

"Harry," I said, takin' a breath 'twixt every couple of words, "if you hear thunder, it ain't rain, it's my heart."

He laughed, real hard. It wasn't that funny. It must have been just his emotions so high.

"We gotta go," he choked out, "in case they were able to follow us."

"Long as there ain't nobody in sight of us right now, let's just go past your house on to the woods where we is campin' and make like we been asleep the whole time," I said.

"What will we do with the buckets?" he asked.

"Hide 'em in the woods over near the cornfield. Most likely they won't be found, but if they was, they'll think whoever done the attack could have dumped them there while they ran along the edge of the field getting away. We'll say we was asleep and didn't know nuthin' about it. We'll clean 'em and take 'em back after school tomorrow."

I started to move, but Harry stood still.

"What's up, Harry?"

"Do you think the cadet who grabbed me, who you hit, would recognize our eyes?"

"Aaw shucks!" I moaned. I went back over the events in my mind. "Harry, would you recognize him?"

"No way," Harry said. "It was too dark and everything was happening so fast. No, Ronson, I wouldn't have the slightest idea what he looked like."

"Then he wut'n know what our eyes looked like, would he?"

We both grinned. I felt relieved and it looked like Harry did, too.

And then we hid the buckets and crawled into our sleepin' bags.

We was all fired up, but we was also awful tired. When my heart quit thumpin' like a steam engine, I went right off to sleep.

IN THE MORNIN', we got up early, took our stuff back to the Hillsons' house, and went to school. We didn't hear nuthin' about what happened at the barracks. Harry, who knowed more about how things worked at the college, reckoned that they wouldn't even report it to the corps administration.

"They've had attacks like this, although more often it was just cold water, for years," Harry told me. "It shows dissatisfaction in the ranks, so is covered up by the cadet officers."

For us, the day just went on like any other. But I felt different. The li'l things didn't bother me like usual. School was work to be done and I knowed I had the strength and willpower to do it. I bored in, done what I had to do, and felt good when the day was over that I done a good job.

When I was almost home, walkin' past the grove of baby trees the school was exper'mentin' with, the winds way up high blowed a white cloud away from in front of the sun and I felt warmth soakin' into my body. The sky was so blue, the clouds so white, and the mockingbird's song so sweet, I jes' stopped and stood still, feelin'. Feelin'.

The sun was made by God, for sure, and maybe it's part of God. It's a lot bigger and stronger and more important than some old man in a white beard sittin' on a cloud, which wouldn't hold him up anyway. I done somethin' to help Elliedine. And that'll help Ma and Pa and the whole fambly if I figger I should tell them about it. And if it stops them fellers, it'll help some young girl somewhere live her life without the misery that come to Elliedine.

The sun was the closest thing to God I could think of, and God must've been with me to get me through that rotten job what had to be done.

I took a deep breath and looked up at the sky.

"Thank ye, Mister Sun," I said. Mister Sun didn't do nuthin' but shine away, but I could swear I seen a little tiny smile in the middle of all that bright. Thoughts was a-tumblin' through my head like 'tater pieces in a stirred soup, but nuthin' stuck. I put my head down and started walkin' on home.

12

JUNE 1940

A day or two later, it turned June and the fresh feelin' of spring turned into heat. I was over at Harry's. He said we gotta return Pete's flashlight, which he'd put in his hidey-hole in our little playhouse behind the Hillsons'.

"Oh, tarnation! I forgot all about that," I said. "He done us a favor and we didn't do right by it."

We took it out and hightailed it over to Pete's. Turns out, Pete hadn't needed it, so he wasn't mad or anything.

What he was was excited.

"Did you hear what happened as a result of your little escapade?" he asked.

"No," Harry and I said, right together. "What?"

"Well, a senior cadet officer found one of the notes you had written when he came in to see what happened. He turned it over to Colonel Cochran, the Commandant of Cadets. The Commandant called for a Cadet Honor Court.

"Of course, Randolph and Green, the guys you call Moley and Whitey, denied it, but they had made the mistake of bragging about it to other guys in the barracks. The guys they had bragged to were required to testify under the oath of the cadet honor code about what they heard. Randolph and Green were found guilty. They were dismissed from the Corps in disgrace. For one thing, they'll never be able to serve as officers in the military in the future. They may even find it hard to get a good-level government job."

Harry's mouth was hangin' open. I realized mine was, too, and I snapped it shut.

"My gosh!" Harry said. "That's great!"

Pete grinned. "Well, just wait," he said. "There's more. Colonel Cochran turned the note and the Cadet Honor Court proceedings over to President Burruss. He's the president of VPI."

"We all know Prexy Burruss," I said, so as he wouldn't take time to explain what we already knew. "What did he do?"

"The university accepted the evidence of the Cadet Honor Court. Those cadets have been expelled from the school. They'll never be back here. It'll go on their school records. That means no other school in the country, and maybe the world, is likely to take them in. Their higher education is pretty much over, and that means they'll have a hard time getting decent jobs for the rest of their lives."

I thought about what I'd do if I was wearin' their shoes. "Can't they just apply somewheres else and not say they ever went here?" I asked.

"I suppose they could," Pete answered. "But even getting into another school, they would have to start over from the beginning. They would have lost two years of their lives. And, on top of it, every time they want to apply for a job, or maybe a loan to buy a house, or anything else where they need to provide a professional history, they will have trouble explaining why there is a two-year gap."

Harry was all lit up, but I could see he had an idea. He was almost jumpin' up and down.

"There's one other thing," he said. "If they ever get accused of being trouble again, the lawyers will track down their history and it will come out. That means they will have to keep to the straight and narrow for the rest of their lives."

"So most likely they won't never hurt no other girl agin," I said, grinnin' and noddin'.

"You're right," Pete added. "It's almost as bad for their futures as if they had had two years in prison."

I knowed I was goin' to tell Elliedine that Moley and Whitey had paid at least in some part for what they done. I argued with myself over whether I should tell Pa and Ma. I figgered it'd go OK with Uncle Sedgwick, but Ma would think I'd taken too big a chance and Pa would say I shouldn't have done it without tellin' him. But then I thought, well, they hadn't done nuthin' at all about it, either cuz they was scared to lose Pa's job or cuz they thought they wouldn't win anyway. Somebody should've done somethin'. And they'd be real glad that Moley and Whitey done got some kind of punishment. My thinkin' was like a two-plate scale where the butcher weighed the meat. I put the weight of how glad they'd be on one side of the scale and how mad they'd be on t'other. I come up heavier glad. I'd tell them all.

That evenin', as we was finishin' dinner, I said I wanted to tell everybody about a happenin'. I was glad my voice had gone down since I turned fourteen, cuz it wouldn't sound like serious stuff if it were said in a little boy's voice.

"I know you're gonna be riled at me for somethin' I done, but I want you to wait me out, all of you, 'til I has finished the whole story. The whole, whole story. Would you do that for me?"

Ma and Pa done look all surprised and serious-like. Uncle Sedgwick and Elliedine seemed interested. Elliedine tilted her head to one side and stared at me real strong.

"All right, Ronson, we'll listen," Pa said, takin' charge.

I started from the beginnin'. "Elliedine done been hurt and wouldn't nobody do anything about it, so I figgered I had to."

Ma opened her mouth, startin' to go at me already. Pa must have seen her out'n the corner of his eye cuz he raised his hand in front of her face. She shut up right smart. Didn't nobody interrupt me after that, although their eyes went from big to squinty and back and their mouths worked somethin' like they was talkin' with no voice.

I told 'em how I learned about the waterin' treatment from Uncle Sedg and how it wouldn't be like puttin' the attackers in jail, but how at least it was somethin'.

And how we thought about somethin' better'n water from the skunk spray on the dog.

And how we found out who they was by gettin' what they looked like from Ellie, which ones they was from their marchin' to church, and their names and beds from Pete.

And how we planned it step-by-step like Elliedine had taught us. How we planned gettin' in and spreadin' tacks, doin' it all timed just right, and gettin' away.

And how we practiced it 'til we could do it with our eyes closed, for real.

And how we saved up money to buy tacks and bought them in sets so they wouldn't be traced.

And how we made up the notes and got the buckets and slurry and stuff together.

And how scared we was, but how we kept ourselves riled up over how they hurt Ellie until we got it done.

"I knowed it wasn't enough punishment for what they done, but I figured somethin' is better than nuthin'," I said.

Thinkin' I was finished, Ma opened her eyes wider 'til you could see the whites all around and opened her mouth ready to go at me. This time it was me who held his hand up.

"I ain't done yet," I said.

I told 'em about the honor court and them gettin' throwed out of the Corps with disgrace on their records.

And I told 'em about Prexy Burruss throwin' them out of the college with that on their records.

And how they couldn't get no more college edication and they'd have a hard time gettin' good jobs or workin' for the gov'mint and all.

I felt scared of Ma and Pa on one side of my gizzard, but on t'other, I felt good to get it all out, like puttin' down a big fertilizer sack I been carryin' on my back.

I ended up tellin' how the cadets couldn't never hurt no other girl agin, cuz their record would come out and doin' it twice would see them throwed in jail.

"OK, I'm done," I said and tears come up in my eyes. "Y'all kin start yellin' now."

But what I heard was the silentist silence ever was. Everbody was lookin' at me like they didn't know who I was, like I was a foreign stranger come to eat dinner with them. A whole minute went by. That don't sound like much, but minutes get long when there's a lot of emotion washin' around.

Then Elliedine jumps up, her chair fallin' over on its back, and grabs me and hugs me tighter'n she ever has. She didn't say nuthin' either. She just hugged and hugged. Then she let go and picked up her chair. I seen her eyes all wet. Uncle Sedgwick broke the silence.

"That's a story like I didn't never expect to hear," he said. "I wouldn't believe it if I read it in a book. And I'll say as God's truth, half the men I was in battle with wouldn't have the nerve to pull that off."

He stopped for a bit, lookin' at me, then went on.

"You done growed into a strong man, Ronson, a good man what knows right from wrong and will fight for the right. You just wait here a minute." And he got up and went to the cupboard where Ma keeps things for special times. He opened it and took somethin' out and come back to me.

Ma gasped.

"Sedgwick, your medal," she whispered.

"Uncle Sedgwick," I said, "I didn't know you got a medal."

"They said it was for bein' brave in facin' the enemy," he said. "But I really wasn't brave. I just didn't have no choice. But you, you went in by choice, Ronson, cuz of what you believed was right. Two fourteen-year-old boys planned and carried out a raid facin' down a whole company of military-trained men. And you won out, accomplishin' your mission and gettin' away. That's a whole lot braver'n and better fightin' than anything I ever did. So this medal is yours now."

And he pinned it on my shirt.

Well, Ma couldn't say much bad to me after that. She just started cryin'. Then Elliedine got up and went over to her and they put their arms around each other and cried together. I couldn't figure what Ma was cryin' at. Was it worry? Relief? Gratitude? Anger? Ain't been a man born that knows what a cryin' woman is goin' at.

Then I looked at Pa. Pa wasn't about to have his thinkin' changed by Uncle Sedg or anybody else. He done his own thinkin'. I still felt scared. I looked at him and he looked at me and I waited.

"Well, Ronson," he finally said. "You done some

very wrong things—you took chances that might have put you in jail and ruined the rest of your life and lost me my job. But you done some very right things—you got justice for Elliedine. We expect a kid to do wrong things. But we don't expect a kid to do right things like you done. On balance, you is more right than wrong. On top of it, it were my duty and I didn't do my duty. You are more of a man than I am, Ronson."

Well, stop my heart! I never heard such a thing. I didn't know what was happenin'. I felt dizzy and everthing was kind of misty, like down in the holler when a fog sets in.

Nobody said nuthin' more. I guess there just wasn't no more to say.

IN THE DAYS THAT FOLLOWED, NUTHIN' more was said. It happened and that was that. It seems to me that folks in the Blue Ridge Mountains pretty much have to take what comes cuz there ain't much we can do about it. Elliedine was smilin' a bunch more and seemed to have healed up a passel. They talk about a glass bein' half full. Well, hers was gettin' filled more. I don't expect it'll ever get to the top now, but it's fillin'. I feel like old times with her now. We can tease each other and laugh and hug. Life has got better.

It hit me one day as I was walkin' acrost the field to Harry's. In the old days, Ellie always seemed to have a little bit of sun shinin' out. It went dark after the bad thing happened to her. But now Mister Sun has put a little bit of his shine back into her. She's beginnin' to glow agin. I stopped, standin' dead still on top of a clod while the thought and all it meant sunk into me. Then I looked up into the sky. I couldn't look direckly into the sun, but I looked a little to the side. "Thank ye, Mister Sun," I said. "I thank ye for comin' back into Ellie."

Now, Harry's a different story. His folks is real good people, but they's more stuck to the rules than mountain folk. They'd be more like to put him under what the po-lice call house arrest than to give him a medal. He decided he wouldn't tell them. He just went on with life like it never happened. But he and I know it did and we is tied together in a close way for always. I think maybe he was braver than I was, cuz he was more scared, but did it anyways. I respect him for that and I told him so. And word got around to other kids, mebbe from Pete Meachum. Anyway, the other kids started treatin' him with more respect. It didn't matter that he couldn't hit a baseball. He was the first chose nowadays. And a funny thing I don't get—he started hittin' the ball. It was like he wasn't scared of missin' no more.

ONE DAY I was over at the Hillsons' when Miz Hillson come up to me.

"Ronson," she said, "I'm going to take Harry to see that new film that's just making the rounds called *The Wizard of Oz*. Would you like to join us? Our treat, of course."

I figgered "treat" meant she was goin' to pay for it. I wasn't sure if I should accept or not, but I wanted to see it real bad. I stammered a little, then decided.

"I ... I ... well ... yes, ma'am. I'd be right pleased."

"And your sister, Elliedine. Ask her to come with us, too. I think she could use a few moments of fun."

Well, I run across the cornfield as fast as a rabbit what seen a hawk shadow and asked her. She got all excited.

"Go tell Ma, Ronson, while I change."

"Change?" I asked. "What for?"

She looked at me like I was a bell in the church what wouldn't never ring and turned and went into the bedroom. In a few minutes, she come out, all decked out in her Sunday-go-t'-meetin' clothes with her hair brushed and a colored bow in it. We walked down to the road and around instead of acrost the field, cuz she didn't want to get her shoes dirty.

When we got to Harry's, Miz Hillson said, "We have to hurry. It starts in about fifteen minutes."

We piled into their new car and she drove down to the Lyric The-ayter.

After we got out of the movie, Elliedine and I both thanked her.

"Miz Hillson," I said then, "that's about the funnest movie I ever seen. I'm gonna remember it always."

She smiled so sweet and happy. I thought about it. Kind folk what does nice things likes to know they succeeded in what they tried. I used to think sayin' thanks was just a po-lite thing you got to say cuz you was taught. But now I see that it's sort of a givin' back. Nobody likes to do work and see it don't come to nuthin'—like gluin' a broke crock only to find it still leaks. When they do somethin' in hopes it helps you, you should say or do somethin' back that lets them know it did.

Elliedine and I turned to start toward home when Miz Hillson said, "Wait. Why don't you have a glass of lemonade before you go? Elliedine, perhaps you could help me to prepare it in the kitchen."

I wandered around the room lookin' in the bookcases that seemed to be on every wall. One book name after another done jump out at me. I wanted to read them all. No wonder Harry talked like he did. He talked like a book.

As I neared the kitchen door, I heard Miz Hillson through it even though it were closed.

"You've seemed so distressed and down lately. Can I help in some way?"

I couldn't hear what Ellie said back. She talks real low when she ain't sure of herself.

I know it ain't right to listen to other folks' private conversations, but I couldn't help hearin'. I moved on around the room lookin' at the next shelf of books in each bookcase. When I went past the kitchen door, I heard Miz Hillson agin.

"I could take you to Christiansburg and let Dr. Showalter examine you to be sure there is no residual injury—or other unwelcome outcome."

This time Ellie spoke up right smart. "No, it's OK." Then her voice faded agin.

After a bit, Elliedine and Miz Hillson come back in with a tray of lemonade and glasses and some cookies. Ellie was walkin' a mite light on her feet, like after you done empty buckets of water you been carryin'. We sat and drank lemonade and I ate more cookies than was po-lite.

We got up to go and—I swow—Ellie done go and hug Miz Hillson.

Walkin' home, Elliedine and I talked about the movie. It brought back the feelin' we had in the the-ayter. She started singin' that song, "Over the Rainbow." She loved it. She sang and smiled her old melt-yer-heart smile and I knowed I'd got my Ellie back. She was gonna be all right with life.

THE SCHOOL YEAR came to a close. My teachers must've liked the way I was thinkin' about school or somethin', cuz they give me good grades for the first time. I got a A and a C, but mos'ly B's, what give me a B average. My folks thought that was somethin' special. They give me a party. Pa fetched a pack of blueberries and bought a quart of milk from the creamery and Ma baked a blueberry pie. They give me all the pie I could eat and all the milk I could drink. And while I was eatin' and drinkin', everbody sat around and laughed and said I was doin' right and stuff. It done make me feel larrapin' good. I do got a awful fine fambly.

It had been a long time since I had felt so stuffed, years I reckon. I got to thinkin' about it. "Pa," I said, "how come you got blueberries? They don't come ripe for another month or two."

"I took a bucket of blueberries we picked last fall from along the edges of the plantin' fields, wrapped 'em in packs, and hid them in the college's freezer."

"Freezer?" I asked.

"The college has a experimental freezer," he said. "They claims ye can put in food that would spoil and keep it fresh for years. Bein' a aggie school, they got to figger out what's the best temperature to keep food froze and how long the food stays good to eat and aggi-culture things like that."

"I don't see how that can be," I said.

"Well," Pa answered, "lookin' at the size of yer belly, ye can see it worked. We know cold slows down spoilin'. Most folks use a block of ice in a insulated box, but them as has money is movin' to get electric refrigerators. Freezers is a step colder, so I reckon it keeps the food fresh even longer. The idea is, at harvest time or slaughterin' time, people can sell some and freeze the rest, and then thaw a little bit durin' the rest of the year whenever they need some."

Uncle Sedge piped up. "The idea's too new for some folks, who say it won't never work. But others is willin' to try it out. Some feller has opened a great big freezer in Cambria, over next to Christiansburg. He rents out shelves. So a bunch of common folks got together and has started what they call a co-op.

"See, big food companies buy big lots of food at

low cost and sell it in little lots at high cost and make a bundle of cash The common folk was payin' for it, as usual. So with this co-op, the common folk can buy a big lot cheap and split it up into little lots for each member. Nobody could do that before there was a freezer to keep the big lot fresh."

"I don't like it," Pa said. "It sounds com-oo-nist to me."

Uncle Sedge put on a smile as wide as a river mouth. "Well, Mason, you is aidin' the com-oo-nists by usin' the college freezer for blueberries."

That sure lit Pa off. He and Sedge had a big yellin' match.

I was sittin' there feelin' fat an' happy like a bear goin' to sleep for the winter, when my stomach gave a little lurch and I couldn't stop a belch from comin' out. Maybe I done eat too much. I felt my face go red. I looked over at Elliedine, but she just give me a great big, beamin' smile. You wouldn't think that was anything, except she hadn't been smilin' like that in a long time. It were the biggest gift I coulda got.

A COUPLE DAYS LATER, I went to Harry's house late in the afternoon. His pa was there back from his teachin' when I come in.

"Dad," Harry said, "Ronson raised his grade average one-and-a-half letter grades over last year."

"That's a remarkable accomplishment, Ronson," Doctor Hillson said.

"Aw, no, sir," I said. "I'm only gettin' B's."

"It's not the current level that's important, Ronson. It's the direction of improvement. See, a common pattern is to start well and gradually slip down grades. A's go to B's and then go to C's. The good students are able to maintain their grades. A's stay A's. But to start low and rise, C's go up to B's, well, that's noteworthy."

He stood there lookin' at me for a minute. Then he spoke agin. "Would you take a walk with me, Ronson?"

Dr. Hillson knew I'd say yes, so he didn't wait for a answer. He set off.

"I want to talk with Ronson alone, Harry," he said over his shoulder.

Harry nodded, but looked a little confused.

We went out across the big front yard toward the road. He didn't say anything. We had got to the pavement and had started along the road when he spoke.

"Ronson, I don't know if you've ever thought about where you want to go with your life, about the limitless number of choices you could make."

I looked at him. I didn't know what he was talkin' about. "No, sir," I said, "I ain't."

"You can be anything you want—if you follow the right path. Doctor, lawyer, professor, business entrepreneur, political leader, explorer—anything. I've had my eye on you for a long time, watching how quickly you learn and your determination to better yourself. You're bright, you're curious, the answers you find go deep, and you put them into practical use. What tops it off, and what led me to talk to you at this point, is how you demonstrated your potential in the actions against Randolph and Green that you and Harry carried out. You showed that you have the determination and strength of character to make use of your talents."

I was havin' trouble followin' all his big words, but forgot all that when I heard him mention Randolph and Green. I felt my eyes grow big.

"You know about that?" I asked, my voice almost squeaky high like before it changed.

"Yes. It was debated in the faculty senate. There was a unanimous vote to back President Burruss's recommendation for expulsion. Of course, they still don't know who carried out the raid."

"Then how do you know that Harry and I done it?"

"Elliedine told Mrs. Hillson. But the exposure stops with us. We are keeping it rigorously confidential."

"Does Harry know you know?"

"No. Not even Harry."

"Then I'll not let on," I promised.

"I didn't think you would."

"Harry was awful brave," I said. "He was stronger than I was, cuz he was more scared."

"I can imagine. I have a far greater respect for Harry than I had. He obviously has remarkable potential. Of course, I've been grooming him for years. But yours is more latent."

My head was swimmin', tryin' to fit everthing in place. But I did realize that he was sayin' very nice things about me and I had to thank him like Ma always taught me. "Well ... well ...," I stammered, "thank ye, Doctor Hillson."

"The way you can thank me," he said with a sideways grin, "is to let me help you develop your potential. Would you agree to that?"

We had passed the entrance to the stadium and were headin' up the hill toward the town water tank. I looked down at my feet, one goin' forward, then the other. I couldn't believe what I was hearin'.

"That'd be all good," I mumbled, not knowin' what I should say.

"All right, then. Well, the first requirement is an interest and curiosity about the world. You have that. Doing well in school is next. You're starting to do that. The final step is the ability to communicate your capabilities to the world. At the moment, that's where you're lacking. So for that, you need to develop two aspects: vocabulary and grammar, two further requirements to getting accepted into the higher education you need. Let's look at them in turn."

I ain't never heard no one talk to me like that. I was understandin' everthing he was sayin' to me now and I knowed he was right. But he was movin' my mind so fast I was havin' trouble keepin' up. Hadn't nobody made my mind go so fast before. He went on.

"A well-developed vocabulary gives you not only the ability to be precise, but also to paint verbal pictures of the images you want to convey. I'll give you an example. I've heard local people call a person they want to belittle a 'dumb son-of-a-bitch.' Now that puts them down, yes, but it gives no clue as to why. They could say he's ignorant, or he's stupid, or he's vain, or he's deceitful, or he's vicious, and on and on. Each of those words paints a better picture of their animosity toward him. You see? By choosing the right words, you conjure the image you want to plant in the mind of your listener."

We was past the water tank with the barns on our left. He stopped and turned around. I guess he knowed he was more'n halfway through what he wanted to say. The big oak trees beside the road was holdin' shady branches over our heads. The gray squirrels was chatterin' at each other as they gathered up nuts. It come to me that most folks is like those squirrels, chatterin' away. They chatters a lot but say only one thing—"get nuts." Then I took that picture in my mind and put it agin the way Doctor Hillson talked. Every word he used meant somethin'.

"The second thing you need is good grammar. The way one speaks also conveys both precision and image. I'll give you an over-simple example to make the point. You say, 'I'm walking to town to buy bread.' But you want to use the word 'only' in the statement. Look at the completely different meanings you get by where you place the 'only.' 'Only I am walking to town to buy bread.' You mean, no one else. 'I am only walking to town to buy bread.' I'm not driving. 'I am walking only to town to buy bread.' That's the only place I'm going. 'I am walking to town only to buy bread.' That's my sole purpose. And the precision and imaging you impart varies for every different mode of grammar you use—the choice and placement of parts of speech, of conjugations of verbs, of declensions of nouns."

He stopped and looked me in the eye. "Do you understand what I have said?"

I looked back. I felt I could look him in the eye, cuz I did understand.

"I get it, Doctor Hillson. To dig up a idea from your mind and plant it in the other feller's mind, you gotta use the right words and say them in the right way."

He smiled real big. "That's it. That's exactly it. Now, if you want, I'll work with you to teach you that."

"That's awful good of you, sir. I'm right smart grateful."

I made a big sigh, lookin' up at the sky. He could see I wanted to say somethin' else, so he waited, all patient like.

"What I don't get is why would you be helpin' me with how to talk, Dr. Hillson? You ain't a English teacher and I ain't your student."

"Then don't think of me as a teacher. Think of me as a coach. I know something you don't, so I guide you to find it. I wouldn't be teaching you so much as just showing you how you can teach yourself. That's really the fundamental purpose of school: not to learn facts, but to learn how to learn. Once you know that, you don't need school."

"But you got lots of important folks to teach."

"Who knows who's important, Ronson? Maybe you'll end up the most important of all. It's just that I'm driven to help young people bring their potential to life. So will you let me?"

"Yes, I will, sir, sure as shootin'."

We'd got back to his house. I was shakin' my head, tryin' to get my mind around what was happenin' here. I still couldn't figure why he'd help me.

I thought and I thought, but I couldn't credit it. Pa and Uncle Sedgwick believe in me. And now a high-edicated man, a doctor what teaches other high-edicated folks to be doctors, believes in me. Just a little hillbilly. Me.

But on second thought, maybe it wasn't so good. Now I can't be just whatever. I has to be somethin', to do somethin', so's they won't be disappointed.

INSIDE, he sat me down and started the coachin' he promised. Harry was listenin', ears perked up like a fox listenin' for a rabbit.

"Your first task, the vocabulary, I think will best come from books of interest to you. That way, it's easy to keep going. Ask Miss Lancaster at the library to help you find the right ones. Tell her you are looking for books that are both interesting to read and that will increase your vocabulary. Keep a dictionary at your elbow and look up every word you don't know. Also, and this is important, look up every word having a strange-sounding use. Many words are used in different ways, and you will both add a usage you weren't aware of before and be less likely to misunderstand when you hear that word being used in the alternate meaning."

He went to the bookcase and reached for a book, handing it to me.

"Here's my spare dictionary. I don't have to use it often, so you can borrow it for a while."

He stood by me thinkin' for a bit, then returned to the bookcase and reached for another book. "Here's a book on grammar. It's to use for reference, not to study as a textbook. When you're unsure of a usage, look it up. I'm here on Tuesdays and Thursdays when Harry gets home from school, so I suppose you do, too. Let's have a fifteen-minute practice when you get here."

"Yes, sir," I said, ever more unbelievin' that this could be happenin' to me. He kept goin'.

"We'll cover parts of speech, verb conjugations, sentence diagramming, things like that."

"But, Doctor Hillson," I said, "I won't never make it the way I say words. I can't say them the same as you."

"You don't have to lose the accent, Ronson, just the bad grammar. Everyone has an accent, because there is no standard. It arises from the way you learned to speak as a child. Thus, every patois other than your own sounds accented to you. I say the British have an accent and they say I have one."

"You mean I shouldn't worry about the way I say words, but use the right ones in the right way?"

He smiled. "That's it exactly, Ronson, exactly." He kept on smilin' at me, kind of like he'd done brought back a strayed calf what was thought lost. I had to speak up.

"There's only one thing, Doctor Hillson. I just gotta ask my pa and ma about this. They're raisin' me and it wouldn't be right to commence a change in my future without they say it's OK."

Doctor Hillson's smile faded, and he looked off at the corner of the room like he expected it to tell him somethin'.

"I tell you what," he said at last. "I'll go with you and tell them about it. It's important enough that we have to make sure there's no misunderstanding. I expect they're home from work by now."

I would have said "don't bother, I expect they'll understand," but he didn't ask me. He told me.

We got up and walked out agin, headin' up toward the water tower and the head of the lane down to my house. Now I was feelin' stranger than ever. The past what he told me and the future what he planned and the right now with him walkin' beside me and him gonna talk to Pa and Ma who he'd never met before. My head was spinny, like when I smoked that cornsilk tobaccy and I was breathin' hard like I done run down a rabbit.

When we got there, I walked ahead, goin' in and callin' my folks. They was in the kitchen, Ma cookin' and Pa and Uncle Sedgwick sittin' at the table with cups of coffee. They looked up and was as surprised as a mouse findin' a cat waitin' outside his hole. I spoke fast before anybody could say somethin' dumb.

"Pa and Ma, this here is Harry's daddy. Dr. Hillson, this here's my pa and ma, Mister and Missus Allen." They all knew who each other was and the names and all, but I had to start it off right. And I didn't want him callin' Pa Mason while Pa called him Doctor. I shouldn't have worried.

Doctor Hillson smiled at them like he'd found a long-lost friend and spoke out, the words almost drippin' with good feelin'. "It's a pleasure at long last, Mr. and Mrs. Allen." He turned to Uncle Sedgwick. "And Mr. Allen. I've been wanting to meet you all for a long time."

Ma was the first to get her breath back. She turned the stove burner off and held out her hand.

"Dr. Hillson. We welcome you to our house, such as it is. Your wife has been so kind to us and our children. Please sit down. Would you like some coffee?"

"That would just hit the spot, Mrs. Allen," he said, taking her hand and Pa's and Uncle Sedgwick's in turn, and then sittin' down with them at the table.

Ma reached a cup, poured coffee, and pointed at the sugar and milk, raising her eyebrows. He shook his head and she handed him the cup.

"If you have a few minutes, I'd like to talk with you about Ronson's future."

They didn't answer, but looked at him, half curious, half worried. They waited for him to go on.

He told them a lot of what he'd told me, but way shorter, about how he'd been watchin' me and how he thought I could do real good if I wanted and how he'd help me if I'd let him. Then he said words what I'd never have put in the same sentence with me, like "smart" and "brave" and "strong character" and "creative" and "dependable" and stuff. I backed up to the wall and pushed against it hopin' it would swallow me. But it didn't.

Ma and Pa sat there with their mouths open, but Uncle Sedgwick found some words. He was direct, as usual. "I can't see why you'd want to do this. We ain't never helped you."

Ma give him a this-ain't-the-way-you-treat-guests look that should've sizzled his hair right off his head.

"Helping young people make the most of their lives is something I care about," Doctor Hillson said. "It's why I'm a teacher. Ronson could do a lot of things with his life, but I have seen how he loves books and learning, and I believe he would be both happier and more successful with a college education. It wouldn't be fair to waste his potential. "

Pa had had a minute to think on it. "I gotta say I

done always thought Ronson was somethin' special, but I ain't never thought about his gettin' that far up in the world. I was hopin' he could get to be a farm supervisor or somethin' like that."

Doctor Hillson just smiled. "I promise you—Ronson can be anything he wants to be."

Now Pa came out all practical. "Well, Dr. Hillson, we's mighty grateful to you, but I see two problems. First is, there ain't no way we could pay you back for doin' all this. And, second, there ain't no way we got the money to send him to college."

"Mr. Allen, seeing a young person shine because of my help is payment enough for me. And when he is my age and living a life that makes him happy and the world a better place, he can help another child in turn. That's where the payback lies. And, as to the cost of college, there's a chance of a scholarship."

Ma spoke up for the first time. "What's that, Dr. Hillson?"

"There are scholarship foundations that would support Ronson financially. They get their funding through the government or donations. Their support doesn't have to be paid back."

This time Uncle Sedg cut in, soundin' real bitter-like. "They's for rich folk. They wouldn't do that for a hillbilly boy."

"Not at all," Doctor Hillson said. "Rich folks

don't need them. They're devised especially for young people without the means to go to school."

"Well, I'll be snickered!" Pa said, raisin' his eyebrows up and openin' his eyes wide.

Doctor Hillson continued, "And, in any event, there are plenty of part-time jobs a student can take to defray the costs. The state schools don't cost a lot and have fine programs. We could probably get him into VPI and he could live at home."

Well, that put a shiver up my spine fast enough. "NO," I said from the back wall, almost shoutin'.

Everybody jerked around and looked at me. I think they'd done forgot I was there.

"I ain't gonna be no cadet," I said, all quiet-like to make up for yellin' out.

Doctor Hillson grinned at my outburst.

"That's no problem," he said. "There's the University of Virginia in Charlottesville and the College of William and Mary in Williamsburg. I suppose you know that William and Mary is the second oldest institution of higher learning in the U.S., just after Harvard, and the University of Virginia was founded by Thomas Jefferson. They're both prestigious and high-quality schools."

Pa held his chin for a minute with his eyes goin' here and there. Then he looked Doctor Hillson in the eye. "Well, I gotta say you make right good sense. I believe Ronson could make it if he really wanted to."

Ma gasped. Uncle Sedgwick grinned and nodded his head.

I melted back into the wall. They all turned to look at each other. My folks and Uncle Sedg couldn't think of nuthin' more to stew about. After a minute, Pa turned to me.

"Is this what YOU want, Ronson?" he asked.

"Yeah, Pa," I said. They was a hundred things I wanted to say, but they was all fightin' to be first and none of 'em could get out.

"We's mighty obliged, Dr. Hillson," Ma said. "You're welcome here any time you see fit to come."

I guess Doctor Hillson knowed his time was over. He stood up, smiled, and nodded to each. "I'll take my leave, then. Thank you for your hospitality. The very good coffee was just the thing after a long day and I enjoyed getting to know you all just a bit."

He turned and left. We was all quiet for a long spell. Nobody knowed what to say.

I was still holdin' my two new prize books as careful as if they was thin glass. I felt I couldn't wait no longer and opened the grammar book. I looked at verb conjugations. They was one called future perfect. I didn't know what a perfect was. But gettin' perfect in the future, well, I figured maybe that was where I was headin'.

THE NEXT DAY I WAS THINKIN' as I walked over to Harry's. I was thinkin' mebbe he'd be mad that his pa would be givin' me attention instead of him. And I was tryin' to figger out why I felt all squiggly inside over seein' Harry. I stopped and stared at the mountains for a while, all pale blue where Mister Sun hit them and purple where he missed. But they didn't give me no answers. And then I saw it like somebody'd struck a lucifer in the dark. We wasn't the same to each other like we always been. I was always stronger and faster and shot better. I shined more than he did, so he always followed me. But now we was about to play a different game. He was always smarter and knowed more'n me. So now I feel like I got to follow him, instead of t'other way around. I'll play by his rules now—leastwise 'til I catches up.

Mebbe it was the sun on the mountains what told me that after all. In my mind, the sun is mighty wise. I looked up toward the sun. I thought, I don't mind. The sun's my best friend and he's got a good heart. He ain't never lorded over me.

"Ye always come every day, Mister Sun," I said, playing my little game. "I never thought about it when I was a kid, but I'm growin' up now and I can see how you're always shinin' light on things to let me see what's what. Well, I thank ye for lettin' me see that, Mister Sun," I told him. But he didn't blink.

With that figgered out in my head, my gizzard settled down and I walked on to the Hillsons'.

I went real slow, cuz I was feelin' both light and heavy at the same time. I walked to the tree that Harry and I played in. I put my arm on a branch. There wasn't no leaves left now. It looked like a gaggle of black bones stickin' up all whitchey way.

Harry come out of his house. He saw me and come over, stoppin' beside me and lookin' up at the branches. A summer breeze come through, stirrin' our hair a mite, but not even little twigs moved. The tree was hard dead.

"It's odd, Ronson," he said. "It's not an airplane or a rocket ship at all."

"I was thinkin' the same thing."

"I don't see how it could have been a great wooden-hulled warship beating through waves with its ochre sails filled by wind."

I laughed at his fancy words. He tried so hard to talk like a book writer.

"You're turnin' into a poet, Harry. No, it's just a rottin' dead mess of branches. In fact, it's right good we didn't keep climbin' it. One day a branch would break and drop us smack on our heads."

We stood quiet. I could tell we was thinkin' along the same path. Harry spoke up agin.

"Ronson, I'm glad my dad is going to work with you. He's been pushing me for a long time. It's sort of like, well, maybe, getting a tight glove on. You push here and it slips a little farther along and then you push there and it slips some more."

"Is that what he's gonna do with me now?" I asked.

"I suppose. I know it'll be good in the long run, but, damn, it gets old while it's going on. I have to say, I've been feeling pretty lonely. Like I was the only one in the world getting squeezed and nobody understood."

"That don't sound purty, Harry. Maybe I shouldn't do this."

"Oh, now that you've gotten your hopes up, you have to." He looked away. It seem like as he wanted to say more but couldn't make up his mind if he should.

I just stayed shut up and watched him. All of a sudden he turned back to me and started sayin' it, fast like. "You have to do it as much for me as for yourself. I need to have someone to share it with. And I couldn't think of anyone I'd rather have."

That made me feel warm inside somehow. He was a good feller.

"That's a load," I said, thinkin' of it as a heavy duty. But he thought I meant a load of crap. He grinned.

"Load or not, you got it."

"I didn't mean to rile ye, Harry. It's jes' all new to me."

"'Just,' not 'jes,'" he said, lookin' at me all sidee-ways like waitin' to see how I'd take it. I knowed he was itchin' to help, even if it stung a mite.

I can see that this is the way it's gonna be, I thought. *He's gonna be doggin' me all the time. Is that what I want? Can I put up with his always bein' ahead of me?*

Then I thought about all the years I been tellin' him things like "Run a little faster, Harry" or "Ye gotta aim a little higher cuz the BB drops as it goes along."

It's just that the shoe done been put on t'other foot. But we can still walk together like always.

"Just," I replied, sayin' it like he tol' me. "It's JUST all new to me."

We both sighed so big it could've been the Huckleberry train puffin'. Seem like as we both seen the change. And we was both good with it.

Harry turned to the tree, grabbed a branch, and tried to shake it. But it stayed rock solid.

"Goodbye, old tree," Harry said.

"Yeah," I said, "We's fourteen now."

"We *are*," Harry said.

"Okay, we *are* fourteen now. And we done been through ..."

"We *have* been through ..." Harry said.

I blinked and swallowed and sighed. "We *have* been through a whole bunch of grown-up stuff. The tree's for children, Harry. It's for children."

EPILOGUE

The "watering" became an unwritten legend at VPI, although most of the time it was just ice water. Its goal was revenge on unfair, sadistic upperclassmen, but it led to a lessening of the viciousness of hazing.

The year following the end of this tale, the U.S. entered World War II. The draft sucked up a majority of the young men who would have been students, and a fair proportion of the faculty. The government stepped in, both unwilling to let universities die off and needing special training facilities. It created the ASTP and STAR programs, using classrooms and faculty, with hundreds of soldier-students from around the nation. It began a Navy flight training program at the Blacksburg airport. It developed the Radford ordinance plant into a major source of war explosives, importing hundreds of workers from around the nation. It began a Civil Air Patrol program in which I was a cadet.

Civilian bomb damage control training and blackout requirements in response to potential German bombing brought the war to Blacksburgers. My father and older brother (until he was drafted into the Navy) were Air Raid Wardens. Practice bombings with bags of flour were carried out by the Navy flight instructors. If you were within fifty feet of a flour bag hit, you had to lie down and wait for an ambulance to rescue you—no matter who you were or what you were doing. Referees were placed all over town to enforce the rules.

Rationing limited meat, sugar, gasoline, tires, whiskey, and other goods. And, like in most places, a black market thrived. Enterprising scoundrels, unfortunately including one of my brothers, traded gasoline coupons for whiskey, whiskey for meat coupons, and meat coupons for gasoline coupons, making a profit on each trade. Along with many Blacksburgers, we raised our own vegetables and chickens and felt less of the privation experienced by big-city folk.

Blacksburg and VPI changed. In the evening, crowds of war workers and off-duty soldiers filled the intersection of Main Street and College Avenue so thick with people hoping to find some activity to release their tension that cars couldn't pass. (The crowds never found their release.) With only one small hotel and few apartment buildings, there was no place for the war workers to stay. The townspeople made available the bedrooms of their sons who had been drafted to go off to fight. There was a mutual culture shock between the small-town locals and the new arrivals uprooted from New York, Philadelphia, and Boston. Everyone remained polite, but each group was rather appalled by the other.

A bit too young for the draft, I delivered the *Roanoke Times* between five and six each morning before I went to school. One morning, Mrs. Winston, whose husband ran a major grocery store in town, called my parents. She didn't get the paper that morning. I was sure I had left it, but my parents told me to take ours to her. When she saw the headlines, she nearly collapsed. Her husband had burned the paper I'd delivered to keep her from seeing the news about huge casualties where their son was fighting. A few days later, the grocery had a sign on the door: "Closed. LT Winston killed in action."

After the war, VPI was again challenged, this time by a huge influx of veterans attending college on the G.I. Bill. Blacksburg was overrun with adult, battle-hardened men from far and wide, including what Uncle Sedgwick would have called Yankeeland. Virginia Tech became cosmopolitan and largely civilian: there was no way the authorities would get combat veterans to wear cadet uniforms. The "Hillsons' house," as I called the home of my early childhood, was razed to make room for a veterans' trailer park.

Blacksburg was never again a cozy little southern college town in the mists of the Blue Ridge Mountains.

AUTHOR'S COMMENTS

The main characters in this story are fictional. The two major events—the issue of cheating on an agricultural experiment and the rape of Elliedine—are fictional. A great many of the other events I either experienced or witnessed, from Harry's tree-of-adventure to cadet watering. One of my older brothers was the contract waterer for a while. One night I drove the getaway car. Some of the minor characters were quite real, like Chief "Highpockets" Sumner, Florence (and sister Mae) Kipps, Margaret Beeks, Professor Boyd Harshbarger, Dr. A.M. Showalter (who brought me into the world), Mac Holdaway, Lucy Lee Lancaster, Dr. Arpad Pap, the garbage wagon driver, and others. They will forever remain with me as live memories; all mention of them are accompanied with deep respect.

Political and social views are intended to represent the views of the region in that era and are not my own views. Indeed, to my surprise, this book turned out to be as much a portrait of depression-era Appalachian culture as the tale of Ronson's search for justice and his emergence from childhood into adulthood. Blacksburg and Virginia Tech also emerged into adulthood in a way. All the observations in the Epilogue are true.

ACKNOWLEDGMENTS

My San Diego Writers and Editors Guild critique group, composed of Janet Travers, Scott Currier, Frank Primiano, and Chris Cunningham, read the manuscript in detail and provided incisive and creative corrections to my many errors. Author and Guild member Margaret Harmon; three of my children, Douglas, Scott, and Dr. Kalena Riffenburgh; my niece Dr. Audrey Riffenburgh; my mephew and author, Dr. Beau Riffenburgh; and my dear friends Thom Munson and Deborah Stilt served as beta readers and provided reviews.

ABOUT THE AUTHOR

The award-winning author R. H. Riffenburgh was born and raised in the Blue Ridge Mountains of Appalachia He has published short stories and poetry. Currently retired as professor emeritus with a PhD (statistics and mathematics) from Virginia Tech, where this story takes place, he has also been a company CEO, government scientist, oceanometrician, Navy undersea diver, ocean sailor, NATO officer in Europe, and medical research planner/analyst. Before retiring, he published four editions of a medical textbook used world-wide and 165 scientific articles and edited two journal series.

Website: robertriffenburgh.com.

www.ingramcontent.com/pod-product-compliance
Lightning Source LLC
LaVergne TN
LVHW041908070526
838199LV00051BA/2540